To Hayley, for giving me the strength to write.

***

Additional thanks go to Jannicke and Zara for reading and discussing early versions of the text.

Finally, thanks to the real Rebecca and Mike, who incidentally have never met.

Chapter 1

My father slammed the door shut behind him, the noise reverberated sharply around the house. Sensing my opportunity – with the place to myself – I ran straight up to my bedroom, opened the third drawer down in my bedside cabinet and searched frantically through piles of old bus tickets, movie stubs and letters stuffed haphazardly back into their envelopes.

I knew it was in there somewhere, I had to keep it hidden from him, to avoid the possibility of an awkward conversation. Eventually I felt its cold metallic casing against my fingers and my expression changed. I slid it out from under some papers and in my state of frustration I prayed the battery hadn't gone flat since last week. I switched it on and as it vibrated sharply I felt a pleasing tingle through my whole body. It still had some power left.

I dialled the only number in the contact list and held my breath for an answer.

'Hello,' said the voice, 'Is everything ok?'

I explained in great detail about the latest row, before begging him – as I had so many times before – to save me from my miserable existence. He gave his usual placatory response, but on this occasion, without the jovial laughter that traditionally accompanied it. He sounded eerily serious – an unnerving silence descended on the conversation. I pulled the phone away from my ear to check the signal.

'Mike?' I said, wondering whether I'd lost him altogether.

I heard a sharp intake of breath, then a slow exhalation, before he calmly spoke.

'I'll be there in half an hour, pack a few things.'

Mike had been a friend of my Mum's for as long as I could remember. They worked at the local hospital together, my Mum as a cleaner and Mike in the IT department. The non-clinical staff had their own recreation room, separate from the doctors and nurses, so the two of them used to take their breaks together. They were virtually inseparable, my Mum said that other staff members used to joke about him being her toy-boy, as he was closer to my age than hers. In reality they were just two regular people who relied on each other to navigate a long shift with their sanity intact.

I couldn't believe he'd actually turn up, but I packed nevertheless. I had a small travel-sized suitcase with wheels, the kind that you can fit into aeroplane hand luggage compartments, not that I'd ever had cause to use it for that purpose. I hastily emptied my underwear drawer into it, then, instantly regretting my decision, carefully removed all the plain white cotton knickers my Mum had bought me for school. I threw in a navy blue hoodie in case I got cold, then carefully folded my best dress and added it gently to the pile. The rest of the free space was crammed with leggings, jeans, t-shirts and two of my favourite pairs of shoes.

The suitcase didn't close, due in part to the haphazard system in which I'd packed it. In fact, to refer to it a system would be overstating it somewhat. I didn't have time to pack systematically, so I grabbed a handful of clothes to remove and searched for another bag. Under my bed I came across my little messenger bag adorned with the picture of a popular Japanese character. The face of 'Kitty' stared directly at me from the front of the bag with what I perceived as displeasure at my decision to run away. I discarded her back under the bed and instead found a plain navy backpack, threw the surplus clothes in – along with my mobile phone – and headed downstairs.

My father had left for the pub after our argument – at least I think he had mumbled something about the pub, it's not easy to decipher his monosyllabic chunter at the best of times. The only excuse I could think of to explain my absence when he returned, was to say I had gone to stay with my friend Lucy for the weekend, which wasn't uncommon. I scrawled a quick note to that effect and left it on the doormat, took up a position on the arm of the sofa in the living room, and twitched the curtains to get a view of the kerb outside.

Minutes later a car pulled up – a dark blue estate with a noisy exhaust, not by design. I ran out with my two bags, dropped them at Mike's feet and gave him a big hug and a kiss on the cheek. He blushed, recoiled slightly and opened the boot of his car to put my bags in, taking a moment to compose himself before slamming the boot shut and getting back into the car. He reached over to unlock the passenger-side door and I flung it open and jumped in eagerly. He turned the key in the ignition, checked his mirrors and edged slowly away from my father's house.

'So where are we going then?' he asked.

'Anywhere.' I replied, checking the side mirrors to avoid being spotted by the neighbours.

I was mainly concerned with not driving past my father as he made his way home from the pub. Mike suggested that we headed to his house for the time being, to discuss what had happened that afternoon and establish just how bad things had become between my father and me. I didn't give any further thought to what we were doing, or how much trouble I might be in if my father found out where I'd gone. I felt safe around Mike, but more than anything else I was just relieved to be out of that house, so I nodded in agreement and sunk back into my seat.

I remained almost silent throughout the short journey to Mike's. It was taking me time to mentally process what was happening, so much so, that when we arrived at our destination my gaze remained fixed out of the passenger side window, my eyes glazed over. Mike's initial reaction was to ask if I wanted to go back, '*God no!*' I thought, but instead I just shook my head and, still not speaking, opened the passenger-side door to get out of the car.

Mike opened the boot from the inside and handed me the keys to let myself in, while he went to collect my bags. I'd been to Mike's house numerous times before so I knew my way around. I switched on the hallway lights, made my way into the kitchen, and set about making a pot of tea.

The door slammed and I heard a voice shout over the sound of the boiling kettle.

'I'll put your bags in your room'.

'I wasn't aware I had a room', I mumbled to myself as I checked the fridge for some milk. I was disappointed to find only the stuff in the red carton, it tasted like water to me but I didn't complain, skimmed milk was the least of my problems at present.

I brought two cups of tea into the living room – set them down on the perversely named coffee table – and sat in Mike's armchair facing the television as he took a seat on the sofa across from me. I stretched my arm out to pick up the remote control from the table but was interrupted.

'Hang on Becky, talk to me about what happened today. What was the row with your father about this time?'

My father had left my mum when I was two years old. I had no memory of him from my early childhood. My mum decided that when I reached secondary school I should know who my dad was, so I could put any questions about him out of my head. At the time I couldn't really see why it was necessary, I'd managed fine up to that point without knowing him. Nevertheless, when I turned eleven arrangements were made for me to start seeing him.

I remember thinking that he was a cold and emotionally distant man. I always felt like he was just doing my Mum a favour by agreeing to the visits. It seemed neither of us really wanted to know each other, perhaps we didn't give each other a chance. We kept up the pretence that we enjoyed each other's company, and continued to spend every other Sunday and one week's annual holiday together.

A few years later I told my mum how I really felt about my father and the time we had spent together. She considered that I had articulated my feelings well enough and told me that I didn't have to see him again if I didn't want to. That was to be the last I saw of him, until a few months ago.

'He's just an idiot.' I exclaimed. 'He never understands what I'm going through at school, just criticises my grades and bans me from the computer even when I have homework to do. He's totally unreasonable. I have an assignment to complete over the summer holiday, I have three weeks left to do it and for some reason he wants me to start it this weekend. It's a bit late for him to start acting like a father when he wasn't around for years.'

'I know things have been tough for you Becky.' said Mike. 'Maybe I can have a word with him and get him to be a bit more patient, provide you a bit more leeway with your homework? I know the school were keen for you to continue your studies as normal but maybe it wouldn't be the worst idea to re-sit this year. You were always going to struggle to cope after what you went through over Christmas.'

It was last summer that Mum had her first stroke. In the days and weeks that followed she changed completely. She was quiet, contemplative, reclusive and lethargic. I had to help her with the housework a lot more, which I didn't mind doing, but in a way it saddened me to have to. I craved for her to shout at me to do my homework, or complain about the state of my room, I even acted out deliberately at times, but she just didn't seem to have the energy to respond as she used to.

Mike had sensed that I was struggling to come to terms with events and was beginning to buckle under the strain of my new responsibilities. In response to this, he came round to our house when he could, helping out in the garden, fixing anything that required it, he always made time for me too. He was there either as a shoulder to cry on when I felt down, or a cheerful distraction when I needed an escape.

Just after Christmas my Mum suffered another terrible seizure, and despite being rushed straight to hospital and given emergency treatment, she didn't make it through the night. I was devastated, not only had I lost my Mum but I'd lost my best friend as well, the only person I felt I could really open up to. I was in a state of shock, I couldn't even cry. The doctor and a grief counsellor asked if there was anyone they could call to be with me at "this difficult time".

Seconds later Mike burst through the doors of the hospital ward. I had no idea how he knew to come, but his timing couldn't have been better. Just when I thought I had nowhere to turn, there he was. I flung my arms around him, streams of tears flooding down my cheeks and soaking the front of his shirt. He didn't say anything, he didn't have to, he was all I needed at that time, all I wanted.

Mike stayed with me until my oaf of a father turned up a few hours later. Evidently the staff had found his contact number on my Mum's patient records. My father also said very little, but his was a far more telling silence, broken only by the kind of small talk and platitudes that usually occur when two people who dislike each other are introduced to one another by an unwitting mutual friend.

A few days after I was living with my father in his house, a mile or so from my old house and further still from my friends and school.

'To be honest I don't really want to think about school right now.' I said, keen to steer the conversation towards a more interesting topic, which at that moment, would have been absolutely anything else.

'Ok, but have a think about what I've said, you know I'm always happy to come into the school with you and chat with your Head of Year about this. I'm going to grab a quick shower, do you want to have a look in the top drawer in the kitchen for a take-away menu? I'm not sure I've got much in the fridge or freezer.'

I found the menus and began to study them intently, Chinese, Indian or pizza seemed to be the main options and I wasn't sure what I fancied. The choice took my mind off the situation with my father though, so I was happy enough just to stare at them blankly for a good five minutes. I eventually selected a pizza, found a pen and circled the one I wanted and put it next to the cordless phone on the coffee table. I then realised I hadn't checked my mobile for a while to see if I had any messages from friends.

As I bounded upstairs to grab the phone from my bedroom I bumped into Mike on the landing. He stood in front of me, fresh out of the shower, naked, except for a towel wrapped around his waist. I lifted my gaze from the floor to make eye contact, pausing momentarily. I noticed a solitary bead of water tracing a line from his shoulder to his chest. I'd never seen him this way before, his body was toned without being overly muscular – not so big as to be intimidating. My brain wouldn't allow my mouth to form the words 'excuse me', but I regained my composure quickly enough to shift closer to the wall to let him pass, before carrying on into my bedroom.

I shut the door behind me, leant back against it and closed my eyes. A perfect copy of the image I'd just witnessed seemed burnt onto the insides of my eyelids, such was the clarity with which I recalled it. I opened and closed them one more time and there it was again. I allowed myself to smile, something I hadn't done that often in recent months. That smile soon dissipated, however, when I found I'd picked up the wrong mobile phone in the rush to get away from my father's house.

I sat on the bed, clutching the old phone that Mike had given me at Mum's funeral. He said I should use it to call him if I ever needed to, he'd even topped it up with credit for me. Mike didn't know my Mum had bought me a smartphone for Christmas a few weeks earlier, I didn't want to belittle the gesture by telling him. The phone was supposed to be for emergencies only but I had called him from it about once a week, usually to moan about my father. It was the best use I could think of for the five pounds pocket money I got each Sunday morning. I realised that in my rush to pack, I must have put my smartphone back into the bedside drawer. At least this meant my father couldn't get hold of me, in fact nobody could, the only person who had this number was currently downstairs, where I could faintly hear him ordering pizza.

I headed down in eager anticipation of the delivery man arriving. I was starving and my mind was fixed on the impending feast right up until the moment I entered the front room and saw Mike sitting there. He was fully clothed of course, in a loose fitting polo shirt and dark trousers, but I was now able to mentally remove those and re-visit the image I had christened 'Shower Mike'.

'You ok Becky?' he asked, noticing my glassy-eyed expression.

'Yeah, fine... sorry, just thinking... nothing important.' I replied unconvincingly.

I could hardly divulge what was really going through my mind. For one it seemed highly inappropriate for me to be thinking of him like that, and secondly I certainly didn't want to jeopardise my new found freedom from my father. I decided that it was just a moment of weakness on my part, and that after a good night's sleep I'd have forgotten what I'd seen and could function normally in his presence.

Mike left the room and returned moments later with some cutlery, much to my bewilderment as I hadn't realised I needed a knife and fork for take-away pizza. The delivery man came and went, and sure enough, there Mike was with two slices of pizza and some garlic bread, carefully dissecting them piece by piece. I ignored the precedent that had been set, picked up a slice in my hands and forced it into my mouth, cheese fat dripping down my chin as I did so.

I devoured my half of the pizza in double quick time, my head angled towards the television throughout. This wasn't because I was engrossed in the documentary Mike had insisted we watch, but rather because I felt I dare not look at him again, in case my staring became too noticeable.

Once we'd finished eating, Mike cleared the table of discarded plastic and cardboard and handed me the remote control. I flicked over to a comedy show on another channel and sunk back into my chair. Mike cast an eye out from the kitchen, unsure whether the programme I had chosen to watch was suitable. He elected not to cause unnecessary tension by expressing those concerns out loud, partly, I suspected, because he wanted to watch it himself.

After an hour of smiles and laughter on my part and awkward facial expressions from Mike – who didn't want to be seen to be understanding the adult humour portions of the show and was further mortified that I might – I decided that it was time for hit the hay. Keen to avoid another embarrassing collision, Mike sent me upstairs first to get ready for bed, remarking that he'd 'join me shortly'.

As I stood in the bathroom cleaning my teeth, I postulated as to whether he meant that he'd join me *in bed*, or simply join me *in the act of going* to bed. I suspected the latter, but the thought kept me occupied such that I spent longer brushing my teeth than I had done since my mum had stopped standing over me while I did so as a kid. I splashed a little cold water over my face, patted myself dry with a towel and headed out of the bathroom and into my bedroom.

I hadn't brought any pyjamas with me so I rummaged around in my little suitcase and found a tattered old t-shirt that I'd packed. I was just about to put it on when I realised I didn't want to be wearing it if Mike *did* come into my room, so I tucked it under the pillow temporarily and got into bed in just my knickers.

I lay silent, motionless, listening to every little noise as Mike entered the bathroom, cleaned his teeth, used the lavatory (a noise I wish I hadn't listened to quite so intently), then opened the bathroom door. I fixated on the sound of each footstep, getting almost imperceptibly louder as they neared my door. I took a deep breath and involuntarily held it. The footsteps passed the door and continued down the hall. Another door opened, not my door, and then closed. I exhaled loudly, fumbled around for the t-shirt under my pillow, wrestled it over my head from my recumbent position and closed my eyes to try to sleep.

'*Maybe one day.*' I thought.

Chapter 2

I woke up to the sound of dogs barking nearby, followed by silence. It was a little too quiet, I had grown used to hearing my dad periodically shouting at me to get out of bed. After the initial joy of being left in peace I began to wonder whether Mike was in the house – I certainly couldn't hear him. I crept over to the door and pressed my ear against it, hoping for the sound of the radio or television downstairs. I decided to investigate further and slowly opened my bedroom door, alas, still nothing.

I crept halfway down the creaky stairs and peered through the gaps in the bannister. There was nobody in the living room, so I called out instead, 'Mike, are you in?'. No response came. I made it to the bottom of the stairs and through the living room into the small kitchen where I noticed a hand written note on the fridge. I made my way over to it and stood, half-asleep and half-naked and took the requisite amount of time to gain enough consciousness to decipher it.

No sooner had I comprehended the words 'Gone for milk' than my brain woke up enough to feel the freezing-cold tiled floor. The icy chill was absorbed initially by the soles of my feet, before suddenly shooting up through my ankles, to my bare thighs and heading, I presumed, for more sensitive areas. I jumped onto one foot, then the other, then hopped and skipped my way out of the kitchen and back upstairs.

This time, as I made my way through the corridor towards my room, I noticed that Mike's bedroom door was open. I couldn't resist a peek and pressed my face against the gap between door and frame, my eyes darting around and absorbing as much information as they could. I listened out for the sound of the front door – or any other sign that Mike was close to arriving home – before heading in for a more thorough look around.

The room was sparsely furnished – just a bed, a large chest of drawers and a single wardrobe. I headed over to the drawers and – with ears pricked – slowly teased open the top one, unsure of what I hoped to find. Much to my surprise, the drawer was full of rubbish, much like my top drawer at my father's house. Most of the junk didn't seem to have any real sentimental value, old name badges from various jobs, some loose change, unopened mobile phone bills, that sort of thing. Just as I was about to close the drawer up I spotted a black rectangular shape, with a fold-out stand, flush to its surface. Face down, but carefully placed, was an eight by ten photograph of Mike, with his arm around a remarkably beautiful woman.

I had no idea who this woman was, I'd never known Mike with a woman, other than my mum and it certainly wasn't her. This woman was almost the same height as Mike, with long blonde hair, slightly curled at the ends. She was wearing a full-length floral print summer dress and heeled sandals. She smiled at the camera and Mike smiled at her. I stared intently at the image of Mike in the photograph, he seemed more youthful than now, but the picture itself didn't look more than a few years old. I'd never seen

Mike smile like that, sure I'd seen him smile plenty of times, but not like that.

I carefully replaced the photo frame face-down and piled everything on top of it, just as it had been, then closed up the drawer with the intention of heading back to my room. Just as I span round from the chest of drawers, however, I noticed a pile of clothes loosely folded at the side of the bed. They were Mike's clothes from the previous day, his socks and a polo shirt. I listened out for the front door again and skipped over to his bedside. I took off my tattered t-shirt and, without further consideration, picked up the polo shirt and tried it on. It felt heavy on my shoulders and the coarse fabric was rough against my skin.

I took a fistful of the front of the collar and brought it up to my nose to try to catch his scent. As I did so, the rough cotton rubbed against my chest, resulting in a simultaneously painful yet pleasurable sensation as it grazed my nipples. I held my breath, pulled the shirt outwards, away from my breasts, then carefully brought it back over my head. I picked up my altogether softer t-shirt and put it back on, before replacing the polo shirt atop the pile of clothes. I hurried out of the room and closed the door to the exact angle I had found it, before scurrying back into my bedroom just in time to hear the sound of a key in the front door.

I finished getting properly dressed, in a knee length denim skirt and clean white t-shirt and composed myself before heading downstairs for the second time. Mike was in the kitchen putting away the few bits of shopping he'd bought, milk and cereal for breakfast and a newspaper.

'Morning Princess.' he said cheerily.

I replied with a more sleepy-voiced 'Morning!' and headed straight for the small round dining room table, much as I would at my father's house at breakfast time.

Instinctively, Mike brought out two bowls, two spoons, milk and cereal, two mugs and a pot of tea and set them on the table in front of me. He smiled in the most energetic way – as frankly nobody should at that time of the morning – before pointing towards a brightly coloured elongated shape on the table. A variety pack of children's cereal, each little box containing a single serving of chocolate or sugar coated tooth-decaying treats. I was a little puzzled as to why he was smiling so eagerly as he pointed at them.

'You used to have these when your Mum dropped you off at mine in the morning, if she had an early shift. Do you remember?' asked Mike.

I did remember, the story sparked a vague memory of sitting at this exact table, in this exact terraced house. I must have been about seven or eight at the time. My tastes had changed significantly since then, I now usually ate much more healthily for breakfast. Understanding the effort he had made I opted to smile back at him before reaching for the box with the least childish looking picture on it.

I felt a little uncomfortable with this memory Mike had of the time we spent together. I didn't exactly want reminders of *cute* things I did as a kid, or how I used to eat all the chocolate cereals first before being disappointed next time I came round to find that only non-chocolate options presented themselves. I wanted Mike to see me as I was now, more grown up, sensible, dependable and a lot closer in height to him than I was back then. As if to make a point, I stood up to pour the tea into our cups, towering over him as he sat eating his cereal. He looked up at me and smiled as I did so – '*mission accomplished*,' I thought.

'So, any thoughts of what you're going to do with me now you've kidnapped me?' I asked jokingly.

Mike choked and spluttered on his cereal.

I'd clearly misread the situation and instantly regretted making the joke. Mike obviously wasn't that comfortable with our current predicament and didn't need reminding that he technically didn't have my father's permission to pick me the day before. We sat in silence for a few minutes. I offered to go back to my father's but Mike rejected that suggestion out of hand, sensing it was an empty gesture on my part.

'Well, to be honest,' he eventually piped up, 'I thought we could take a little trip away for a few days, to take your mind off things.'

This time *I* nearly choked on *my* cereal.

'Really? Where?' I asked. Not that *where* really mattered to me at that time.

'London.' said Mike, 'I haven't been for a while. Work sent me to this really nice hotel a few years ago with a pool, a gym, a nice restaurant and everything. I made a mental note to go back sometime.'

'That sounds amazing.' I responded, before eating my cereal even more hurriedly.

'Slow down, slow down, you won't get there any quicker by giving yourself indigestion.' said Mike. 'We'll pop to the big supermarket on the outskirts of town and pick up any provisions we might need, grab a sandwich or something for lunch while we're there and head straight off.'

'Don't you have work?' I asked, slurping the dregs of milk from the bowl.

'Actually I took voluntary redundancy. Yesterday was my last day working at the hospital. The IT department is being outsourced and they're transferring most of the workload to the Local Health Authority. So I have a bit of time on my hands and don't have to look for anything right away.'

'And you can't think of anything you'd rather do with that time than take me on a trip to London, Mike?'

He smiled wryly and I realised I should shut up before he started questioning what – to my mind at least – was clearly a most excellent use of his time and redundancy money.

'One more thing,' said Mike, 'I know I'm not really old enough, but I think maybe it would be sensible if you call me *Dad* instead of *Mike*, just when we're in public. Just in case anybody gets the wrong idea. As long as you're comfortable with that?'

I fully understood the reason he'd made the suggestion. I didn't have any specific problem referring to him in that way, but I had hoped to alter the dynamic of our relationship and this would surely be a stumbling block. On the other hand I didn't want to cause him any trouble, so I reluctantly agreed.

We finished our breakfast and I sprinted upstairs to clean my teeth and begin packing my toiletries back into their bag. I couldn't really believe my luck, I was keen to get closer to Mike and a few days away together seemed like just the way to do so. Cooped up in a hotel room he couldn't avoid me if he wanted to. There would be many more awkward post-shower meetings, for both of us. I suddenly became extremely self-conscious about my own body. I paused from packing toiletries and stared into the bathroom mirror at the pale, skinny girl looking back at me.

I took off my t-shirt and pulled my bra straps down over my shoulders before wrapping a towel around myself to see how the strapless look would work for me. I ruffled up my hair a bit and tried to pin it on top of my head with one hand. At this point I realised how ridiculous I looked and let it fall back over my shoulders. I stared again, blankly, into the mirror. This pose looked far more natural and I allowed myself to smile at the seemingly care-free girl who looked back at me.

I collected the rest of my toiletries and headed back into my bedroom to pack the few items I'd taken out since arriving, before bringing the case downstairs and placing it by the door. Mike was just getting off the phone and had managed to book the same hotel he'd stayed in before. I caught the tail end of the conversation and listened eagerly to make sure it was true.

'Check in time from 3PM, that's great. Ok, thanks for your help. Bye now.'

'All sorted?' I asked cheerily.

'Yep, we were lucky though, they only had a few of those particular rooms left.'

Somehow I wasn't surprised, my luck definitely seemed to be in at the moment. I sat on the sofa and began making a list of the things we might need for our trip. When repacking my suitcase moments ago, I'd stashed the old navy swimsuit I'd inadvertently brought under the bed, so that I'd be allowed to buy another.

Mike picked up my bags for me and stepped outside as I followed, he reached back over my shoulder to close the front door and momentarily pinned me against the wall as he did so. This caused me to hold my breath for those few seconds and wait until he was halfway down the driveway before I finally exhaled and followed him towards the car. If I was planning on being intimate with this man I was really going to have to learn how to breathe while he was within a few feet of me. As he started packing our bags into an already untidy and somewhat full boot I jumped up and sat on the little wall that separated the front garden from the pavement.

Any excitement I felt was certainly tinged with trepidation, not about the journey ahead, but what might be waiting for me on my return. What if my father found out I wasn't at my friend's? Why does everything at his house have to be so awful? Could I really return to living with my father when this trip was over?

Mike closed the boot and turned to see me looking mournful as I sat on the garden wall. He walked over and perched himself to the left of me – in an inadvertent unnaturally close proximity, with our hips touching – but he didn't dare shuffle away at this poignant moment. He turned to face me just in time to see a solitary tear make its way from my right eye and trail down the crevice at the side of my nose towards the corner of my mouth.

Just before the tear reached my top lip Mike extended a finger, in order to catch it and wipe it away. Unfortunately for him, fully aware of the tear's path towards my mouth I had already began protruding my tongue to intercept it. In an impromptu race, fraught with embarrassment and sexual tension – at least on my part – the result was a dead heat, ending with my tongue licking the tip of Mike's finger. He pulled his hand away sharply and I let out a nervous laugh, which allowed him to feel at ease and follow suit.

Before we knew it there we were, sitting on the wall, both laughing like a couple of idiots. There was no need to discuss what had made me cry in the first place, so we simply stood up, got in the car, and set off on our trip.

Chapter 3

As I stood in the doorway of the supermarket, the bright fluorescent light that surrounded me gave my skin a hideously unappealing blueish-white tinge. I shuddered at the sight of it and left Mike wrestling with the trolleys while I headed for the nearby racks of magazines. I flicked through a couple of the more grown-up titles emblazoned with promises of 'unlocking your partner's potential in bed' and tips for 'fulfilling your sexual desires', before heading to more suitable territory as Mike arrived at my side. I found a teen magazine with the feature article 'Five steps to snag your man' and threw it into the trolley, before marshalling Mike towards the all-encompassing Summer section that supermarkets have at this time of year.

'I didn't bring my swimsuit, can I get one from here? It won't be expensive.' I asked politely.

Mike nodded and suggested I look at those myself while he took care of hay-fever tablets, sun lotion and plasters from the list. He seemed intent on packing an entire first-aid kit. His overzealous preparedness amused me, but also cemented my view that I would always be safe around him.

I stood in front of a rack of swimsuits and bikinis, of which there were far more of the latter. I'd never owned a bikini before but I like the idea of shedding my plain navy swimsuit in favour of something a little more risqué. I wasn't quite ready for the piece of floss with the four material triangles, but I spotted a bright yellow two-piece I liked the look of. Finding a small enough size was trickier butt my persistence paid off and I scrunched up the new bikini in my hand and prepared myself for the potentially awkward task of sneaking it into the trolley without Mike's intervention.

I needn't have worried as he barely batted an eyelid as I chucked it on top of the magazines. Perhaps he just averted his gaze deliberately, so as to not have to be drawn into a conversation about what constitutes a suitable swimming costume for a teenage girl. I spotted the sun lotion, hay-fever tablets and plasters in the trolley, along with some sandwiches and snacks. All that was left now, as far as I was concerned, was a cheap pair of sunglasses and some travel sweets.

Mike stood patiently while I tried on every pair of sunglasses on the stand, even trying the same pair more than once, just to make sure he definitely wasn't paying attention. Each time I turned I was met with the same fixed smile that seemed to say "They all look good but can we hurry up?". I finally settled on a pair that covered up more of my face than usual, but I figured that doing so would help conceal the age gap to my companion.

We queued at a till and I threw in a few packs of nearby boiled sweets, the kind that only work as travel sweets or to be offered around at Christmas, since nobody could ever eat the whole pack in one go. We waited patiently as the cashier scanned another customer's items, and with both our hands perched on the back of the trolley, I began to look around. This was the first time up to this point that I'd paid attention to the existence of other people in the supermarket. Prior to this I had been solely focused on checking off items from our list. I noticed customers gawping at us, perhaps I seemed a little too enthusiastic about being in a supermarket with my 'Dad' at 11am. Of course I might have just been imagining it, but I wasn't about to sulk, or walk off behind the tills and play with my phone in keeping with the other teenagers in the store.

I packed up our shopping while Mike paid, then we headed out of the supermarket with our own respective bags, mine with the bikini and travel sweets, Mike's with everything else. The sunglasses were, by this point, on my head, with the tags strewn across the packing area of the till. We walked across the busy car park and I felt like our journey was finally about to begin. Or at least it would after Mike had filled the car with petrol, as he reminded me when I vocalised my excitement.

I wandered around the petrol station while Mike filled up. It was like a miniature replica of the shop we'd just been in. I couldn't find anything worth browsing so I met Mike in the queue at the tills.

'Just petrol?' said the cashier.

'Yes just the petrol, thanks.' Mike replied.

'Number?'

'Oh erm, it's the blue estate, number three is that? I can't see with the light shining on the sign.'

'Yeah that's three, off on holiday?' asked the cashier in an overfamiliar tone.

'Sorry?' said Mike.

'Are you heading off on holiday? I noticed all the bags in the back. I'm going next week, Magaluf.'

'Oh right, er, just taking a trip for a few days with er... my daughter.'

The cashier looked down and left to a smiling me, then back up at Mike.

'That's £44.53 then.' Said the cashier, preferring to get down to business with a queue forming behind.

Mike inserted his credit card and waited for the prompt for his PIN. As he did so the cashier looked at me, then at Mike again. Had we run into the world's most observant petrol station cashier, or was it that obvious that we weren't, in fact, dad and daughter? I was 5ft 4, with a pale complexion, long blonde hair and green eyes. Mike didn't look old enough to be my biological parent, plus he was just over 6ft, medium tan, with short dark brown hair and even darker brown eyes. I guess there could have been some kind of mix up at the hospital, you do hear stories.

'Have a nice trip then, sir.' said the cashier, almost suspiciously.

Mike withdrew his card from the machine, smiled awkwardly and scurried out the door with me a few yards behind. As we got into the car Mike turned to me and muttered the dreaded words 'Are you ok?'

Of course I was ok, I was more ok than I'd been in a long time. Often the only reason someone asks whether you're ok is because *they*, are in fact, not ok. I calmly told him that I was better than ok, and that he should ignore what the cashier in the petrol station thought about us going away together. It's not like we're strangers that met off the internet, I reminded him. Still, Mike suggested we concoct a more believable back story that would stand up to scrutiny, in case we ran into any more overly-interested waiters, cashiers or desk clerks.

It was soon decided that I was adopted as a baby by Mike and his ex-wife, whom he wished to be named Marie, for a reason that was unclear to me. I didn't want my adoptive mother to be called Marie, there was a girl at school called Marie, I didn't like her. Mike was, however, quite insistent on this point, unusually so. Regardless, this story gave Mike peace of mind, it explained away stark contrasts in our appearance and meant that while in public, he could call me his daughter and I could call him 'Dad', without either of us stumbling over our words. We pulled away from the supermarket petrol station with the air cleared, satisfied that nothing else could spoil our trip.

***

The journey to London began relatively uneventfully, we didn't seem to be getting anywhere particularly quickly and every time I tried to strike up a conversation I was met with initial silence, followed shortly by a 'Sorry, I was just concentrating on the road.'

Can I at least put the radio on then?' I asked

'Just let me concentrate on getting onto the motorway.' replied Mike.

Fifteen or so minutes of silence later, we made our way down the slip road onto the motorway and I was able to switch on the radio. Having done so I was a little disappointed to be greeted by the sound of some decidedly middle-of-the-road rock music. I frantically clicked through the pre-set stations, Easy Listening, Talk Radio, Smooth, Classical and Sports. *'How could anyone have 5 pre-set station buttons and no pop or dance?'* I thought. I had to remind myself I was sitting in the clapped out blue estate of a 30-something bachelor.

I rifled instead, through a few CD's I'd seen scattered about the glove box and in a compartment in the passenger side door. Old crooners and Dad-Rock seemed to be the order of the day. I looked over at Mike – who was still concentrating on the road – and decided to chance my arm at manually tuning the radio to my favourite station. Two minutes of hissing was occasionally punctuated by talking and adverts, until finally some dance music blared out of the speakers and saved me from the dullest car journey of my life.

Mike reached over and turned the volume down slightly, citing his need to 'concentrate on the road'.

It suddenly occurred to me we'd been driving for about half an hour and yet I hadn't opened the travel sweets I'd bought in the supermarket. I looked around by my feet for the bag, but it was nowhere around.

'Do you know where the sweets are?' I asked.

'Erm, I think they're in one of the bags in the boot, but...'

It was too late, I only heard the first part of that sentence before undoing my seatbelt and diving through the gap by the centre console, with one knee on the back seat and my head perched by the rear headrests looking around for the bag. The precarious way I was positioned and the urgency with which I'd leapt back there, had caused my skirt to ride up significantly. I felt the need to straighten it first before I set about making a lunge for the carrier bag that I'd spotted over to one side of the boot. As I looked round to see what I was doing my eyes met Mike's in the rear view mirror.

'I thought you were concentrating on the road?' I asked playfully.

'I was just making sure you were ok.' said Mike.

'And did I look ok to you?' I asked, a sudden rush of blood causing me to lose all inhibitions.

'Just hurry up and sit back down.' said Mike, less flustered than I'd hoped.

I yanked my skirt down to cover my bum, turned back around to grab the carrier bag and shuffled my way back to the front of the car.

I opened up the packet of boiled sweets and plunged my hand in to grab a few. They were individually wrapped and I wanted to make sure I got the best flavours. 'Ooh, a green one.' I muttered to myself, hoping it would be apple flavoured. '*Euch, lime, whose idea was lime flavour?*' I thought.

I sat quietly, ruefully sucking on my lime flavoured sweet so as to avoid further distracting Mike. Eventually I had finished it and found a nice safe red one, I crossed my fingers for strawberry and my luck was in once again. I decided to sort the safe from the potentially harmful flavours in the bag.

'Mike... do you like blacks? Cos I don't.'

Mike spluttered slightly, seemingly taken aback by my question.

'Well, I er... I don't have any black friends or anything, but I certainly don't have a problem with any races or religions.' he replied awkwardly.

After a momentary pause and with a furrowed brow I expanded on my question:

'The sweets Mike, do you like the black sweets? I think they're liquorice flavour.'

'Oh, God... right, sorry, yes I don't mind the black ones.' said Mike.

'Open wide then.' I demanded.

I leant over and popped the black sweet I'd just unwrapped into his mouth, he gripped it firmly with his teeth to avoid any more unnecessary licking of each other's fingers.

I sat back in my seat and smiled to myself about our little misunderstanding. I wondered if it reflected badly on me, did he really think I would be asking something awful like that? Maybe it was just further evidence that he considered me less well-informed, even childish or immature. I was going to have to do my best over the next few days to convince him otherwise. Circumstances had dictated that I grow up fast, I felt I was more mature than any of the other girls in my class. I considered ways in which I could prove to Mike he was in the company of someone he could talk to as an equal.

We stopped briefly at a motorway service station, to use the facilities and eat the food we'd bought that morning. We felt particularly proud of our preparedness, especially as the same sandwiches were twice the price by the side of the motorway. We made idle chit-chat as we ate, since the engine, and thus the radio, was switched off. Once we'd refuelled ourselves and the car, we set off again quite quickly.

I sat quietly again, still contemplating the nature of our relationship, right up until the moment we hit the centre of London. The vast openness of the Kent countryside was replaced by giant glass buildings, a sort of greyish haze across the sky, and more cars than I'd seen in a DIY store car park on a bank holiday weekend. I shrank down in my seat, partly to get a better view of the tops of the buildings and partly in reverence to the awe-inspiring cityscape before me.

We passed one glorious building after another, until we came to a huge glazed monolith with a sign on top. The car slowed slightly and at the last minute, veered into a tiny access road and underneath the bowels of the building. The shift from light to dark caught me off guard and my eyes took a few moments to adjust. By the time I could focus them again we had come to a halt in front of the grand entrance to the London Metropolitan Hotel.

Chapter 4

A man in a dark blue suit with gold trim walked round to my side of the car and opened the door. Countless sweet wrappers fell at his feet and without complaint, he bent down to pick each of them up one by one.

I stepped out of the car and made my way around to the boot to get my bag. As I did so I noticed another man in an identical dark blue suit with gold trim standing by a large metal cage. I quickly looked back toward the first man, in case I was seeing double, he came into view as he stood up, having put all of the sweet wrappers in his pocket. Mike opened the boot from the driver's seat, but as I reached inside, a booming voice stopped me in my tracks.

'Please Miss, allow me,' said the second dark blue suited man, 'you can go right through to reception'.

I turned to look at Mike who had walked round the front of the car and was handing the keys to the first dark-blue-suited man. Mike then gave me a little sideways nod of the head to beckon me over and I joined him on the kerb. He assured me the impeccably-tailored men would park the car, get all our bags and bring them up to our room for us. I think I'd have preferred to keep my bags with me but I didn't want to seem awkward or unknowledgeable of hotel etiquette.

We walked through a pair of sliding doors into a beautifully lavish reception area. Bright sunlight beamed in through the glass sides of the building, the floor was shiny black, speckled with flecks of silver and pewter. Fresh flower displays were dotted throughout and guests sat drinking coffee in little armchairs over to each side of the main desk. I could also see – and partially smell – the pool from the main foyer. I politely asked Mike if I could go and have a look while he queued at check-in.

I pressed my nose against the window, the pool water looked clear and blue, warm too if the condensation on the window was anything to go by. I moved back a few centimetres and wiped the moisture from the tip of my nose. Some guests sat around the pool on sun loungers and were reading books or working on laptops, some disappeared into two doors at the back of the pool area, the contents of which were unclear to me.

I turned to see Mike at the reception desk and I scurried over to be by his side. By the time I arrived he was already mid-conversation with a member of staff.

'Ok, can I get a credit card to swipe for incidentals?' said the lady behind reception with 'Julie' on her name badge. Mike handed over his card, she swiped it and began pressing buttons on the keyboard.

Julie was a stout woman, in her mid 40's I would guess, with far too much make up on and her hair scraped back over her scalp. She spoke with an insincere, soft yet forceful voice, as if giving passive-aggressive instructions to a naughty puppy. She typed away on the keyboard with a sense of self-satisfaction, every keystroke was elaborate and accompanied by a jaunty tilting of the head. Julie seemed to me to relish her position of power, as she no doubt saw it. Gatekeeper, guardian of the key cards. If your name wasn't down, you definitely weren't coming in.

After a few minutes more of tapping and swiping, form-filling and signing, we were done. Mike was handed back his credit card, followed by two more identically sized key cards, one of which he put in his wallet and the other he slid along the top of the desk to me. I thought it was a little strange, I was unlikely to leave his side at any point, but I guess you can't be too careful – 'always handy to have a spare' I mused. I smiled at him and picked it up off the desk and held onto it as I had no pockets or purse to put it in. The receptionist pointed towards a large open staircase in the corner and we walked towards it. I still felt a slight unease at being separated from my suitcase.

'We're on the second floor so it's easier to walk up here than use the lifts.' said Mike.

I nodded quietly in agreement and we climbed the ornate staircase together and stood in front of the sign at the top. I checked the key card in my hand, it was tucked into a small cardboard wallet with the number 238 on it. The sign instructed me to turn right at the top of the staircase. About halfway down the corridor and with Mike in tow, I found the corresponding door. I turned back to Mike for reassurance.

'That's the one, in you go then.' he said.

I inserted the key card slowly into the slot and removed it, a small light turned from red to green and flashed, giving off a small beep as it did so. The handle which was previously stuck firmly, now allowed me to push down on it, and the door opened. I stepped inside and looked for a light switch as the curtains had been drawn fully closed. As I searched, the door slammed sharply behind me. I span around, in the dark, the last shard of light from the hallway had gone, I couldn't see or hear anything.

I found a light switch to my right on the wall and the bathroom light came on, giving me just enough light to see the rest of the room. I turned back to look for Mike in the doorway but he was nowhere to be seen. Confused at first, I found more light switches and turned them all on to see if he had snuck past me in the commotion and could be found in the bedroom area. Still no sign. Then I heard another loud slamming door that echoed slightly and sounded like it came from elsewhere. I was somewhat disoriented by what came next, a knocking sound coming from another door, next to the wardrobe. The knocking was followed by a familiar voice.

'Becky?.. Becky can you hear me?'

'You need to turn the little lock to the right.' said the familiar voice.

I did as instructed and turned the small silver lock to the right on the door next to the wardrobe. As I did so it swung open out of my room and in its place stood Mike.

'Ta-da,' said Mike, 'adjoining rooms. How cool is that? Anyway I need to use the loo and freshen up after the drive so you settle in and have a nose around your room.'

The door next to the wardrobe slammed shut and I instinctively fell back onto the bed behind me. How could I have been so stupid as to think we would actually be sharing a room? Of course we wouldn't – of course he wouldn't allow that. My heart sank as it became clear that we wouldn't be as intimate as I had hoped during this trip. I was desperate just to be close to him, to feel his breath on my skin. I was disappointed, angry even, mostly at myself for ever believing there was a possibility of that happening.

I was still lying flat on my back atop the bed a minute later when Mike returned.

'Our bags have arrived, they all came to my room so I told the chap just to leave them with me and I'd bring yours in to you.' said Mike, ignoring the fact that my exasperated self hadn't yet answered, or indeed responded to his presence in any way.

He left my suitcase and backpack at the bottom of my bed and headed back into his own room, this time being careful not to slam the door and disturb me from whatever malaise had come over me. I stood up and walked over to the door by the wardrobe and flicked the silver lock, this time to the left. Realising what I'd done Mike shouted through the door to me.

'I've made reservations in the restaurant for 8pm, is that ok, Becky?'

'Yeah that's fine.' I shouted back.

'Ok, well grab a shower or whatever and relax for a bit, I'll knock for you again at about 7:45.'

The time was now just before 5pm – that gave me a little under three hours to get ready. After my initial disappointment concerning our living arrangements, I decided to not fixate on the negatives and keep trying. I would indeed grab a shower, but there would be no time to relax afterwards, I had to make the most of the time available to make myself look as amazing as possible for our romantic dinner together.

I got changed out of my t-shirt and skirt and kicked them to one corner of the room. I headed into the bathroom, turned on the shower and left it to run briefly – to make sure it was warm enough – while I took off my bra and knickers. I looked at myself again in the mirror. This mirror was less forgiving than the one at Mike's house and the closer I got to it the more pockmarked my skin seemed to become.

I peeled back the shower curtain and stuck a solitary arm out in front of the powerful jet of water from the shower head. The hotel was relatively warm and the bathroom even warmer, but as the water rushed through my fingers and splattered my forearm, I decided I could stand to be warmer still. I turned the temperature dial a fraction further to the right and stepped into the shower.

The increased heat hit me instantly as I stood facing away from the shower, the back of my neck taking the brunt of the pressure, causing small goose-bumps to form in a way that usually only extreme cold could provide. I could feel my skin reddening and as I turned to relieve the tingling pain I only managed to redden my chest just the same. I ducked my head under the stream and my hair gave me momentary solace before eventually my scalp too felt a light burning sensation.

Before long, any mild discomfort was gone, partly because my body had got used to the temperature of the water, partly because my mind had wandered to my counterpart on this trip, more specifically in the guise of 'Shower Mike'. As the soft hotel water enveloped my skin, I imagined Mike's hand's instead running over my gentle frame. The change in temperature as I moved different parts of my body in front of the stream of hot water played tricks on my mind, allowing my hands to become his hands and with every stroke of my fingertips I became more and more convinced of his presence.

I grabbed for some shampoo and began washing my hair, running my fingers through the long blonde strands which clumped together when wet. Again I managed to convince myself it was Mike's hands that were now massaging my scalp. With my eyes firmly closed I reached for the shower gel and continued my routine.

Before long I began to feel dizzy. The steam that had built up in the enclosed bathroom – combined with the water now seeming hotter than it had been – led me to sit down on the floor of the bath. This not only served to stop my legs from buckling, but also allowed the water to cool down an additional degree or two and strike me less firmly – in my new position – a few feet further away from the shower head.

Soon, the warm feeling enveloped me once more. I was sat upright with my back to the moderately cool tiles, my legs crossed and my mouth wide open in order to fill my lungs with what little air was left in the bathroom.

My field of vision seemed to narrow, I focused on the taps at the other end of the bath, then they too blurred and I was left with visions of 'Shower Mike' once again.

I remained stationary for a matter of seconds and – without realising – allowed my mouth to fill up with warm water. My brain sensed its presence and as a physiological reflex I leant forwards slightly and pushed the water out with my tongue, causing a small cascade to run down my chin onto my chest, between my breasts and over my stomach. I felt a little disgusted by the sight of it and leapt back up in order to wash my torso again with clean water.

As I did so the blood rushed to my head and I planted one hand firmly onto the tiled wall in front of me to steady myself. This second dizzy spell eventually passed and I was finally able to rinse my hair and step out of the shower.

I opened the door and the comparatively cool air rushed in and breezed past my body. It seemed to make a lap all the way around me, hugging every contour and crevice, before heading back out through the door. I quickly reached for a towel and wrapped it tightly around myself. I patted my feet dry on the bath mat, put an extra towel around my hair and made my way back into the bedroom area in order to make myself look beautiful for my 'date'.

Chapter 5

I had sat on the bed for a while to cool down and catch my breath after my shower. I'd opened the window to try to get some fresh air into the room, as the extractor fan in the bathroom was failing to do its job. As I sat, I surveyed my surroundings in more detail, I hadn't had the opportunity to look around until now. I had plenty of time to get ready for dinner, so I decided to read the assortment of paperwork tucked inside the red leather folder on the desk.

Inside, was a selection of menus, for room service and the restaurant, as well as a separate entry for breakfast. We were to dine in the hotel restaurant that evening so I had a cursory glance at what I might order that was sufficiently grown-up. My eye was soon turned by the bar menu, which included a spirits section with prices I could only assume related to an entire case of the stuff. I hoped I didn't accidentally order a £4000 cognac after dinner, although I suspected there wasn't much likelihood of that.

The last leaflet I looked at had a map of the first floor of the hotel, as well as one of the floor we were on now. Confusingly, the two maps were completely different shapes, so it was hard to work out where we were in relation to the swimming pool or restaurant. Having thumbed through the folder long enough, I decided to open every drawer and cupboard in search of more entertainment. I wanted to make the most of having my own hotel room, I rarely had the chance to explore like this.

I found a hairdryer in one drawer, which would be handy if we were in a rush one morning, as well as the remote control for the television. In the wardrobe, amongst the hangers, was a tiny electronic safe. I pressed a few buttons and it beeped angrily at me, causing me to move on. In the bathroom was a selection of little soaps, shower gel and shampoo in tiny bottles and a shower cap. I'd never seen anyone use a shower cap before but I mentally etched it onto my to-do list for while I was here.

Finally, back in the bedroom, in a little cabinet next to the bed, was a bible. I opened it up and saw an inscription which read 'This Bible has been placed here by The Gideon's International' under which someone had scrawled, 'Thanks Gideon, it propped up the wonky leg on the chair by the window.' I was bemused by both of these statements, but only one could be successfully tested at present, so I walked over to the chair and prodded it. Alas it was obviously a different chair, as it needed neither a Bible nor any other device to keep it from wobbling.

My thoughts finally turned to our plans for the evening. I wanted to make a good impression at dinner. This was my first chance to be seen out with Mike, in a formal setting. I remembered the title of that article, 'Five steps to bag your man.' I hastily grabbed the magazine from my bag and studied the contents page to navigate directly to it. I read the first few paragraphs of the article out loud to myself.

'Step one: Get him to notice you.

Once you've identified the guy you like, it's time to find out whether he likes you too. The best way to do this is to make eye contact and smile, then see whether he reciprocates. Hopefully, as well as making eye contact, he'll want to look at the rest of you in more detail, so wear something that makes the most of what you have to offer, but isn't too revealing. Finally, as an extra tip, science has proven that men are attracted to a woman's bare neck, so consider wearing your hair up, if appropriate, or alternatively wear it to one side. This is all but guaranteed to make him look at you differently.'

'*Perfect!*' I thought, as I picked up my bag from the foot of the bed and set it beside me. In there, amongst all the tops and skirts, was the saving grace of my wardrobe – my pièce de résistance – my very own little black dress. Of course, if anyone had known that's what it was at the time, they'd never have bought it for me. I carefully peeled it from the bag and draped it loosely across a hanger, over the top of the wardrobe door.

The dress was very plain in style, tapered to the waist and just above knee length, with a square neck. It fitted me well and simulated curves where, in reality, there were none. Of course, a padded bra also helped create the illusion that the front of the dress held anything of note. I had only worn it once before, in vastly different circumstances, and on that occasion I didn't really care how I looked in it.

I paused in reflection for a moment and closed my eyes, as I always did when thoughts of my Mum surfaced. I knew she would be happy as long as I was happy. She'd always liked Mike and had been bitter towards my father for many years, only burying the hatchet for my sake. I mumbled a few words to her under my breath and carried on planning how to accessorise my outfit for the night.

Despite leaving in a hurry, like all girls, I had the good sense to bring my favourite pair of shoes and handbag along with me when I'd left my father's house. One of the two pairs of shoes I'd selected were my black kitten heels. They were the only heels I had, the only ones I was allowed, but they took me from 5ft 4 to 5ft 6, which I was sure was vitally important in making me look older than I was. The shoes were a little frayed around the edges, they were, after all, my school shoes during term time, but paired with the little black dress they'd work just fine. I grabbed my trusty black padded bra, some matching knickers and 60 denier tights and put them on before sitting down at the little desk to apply my make-up.

I didn't wear make-up often, I wasn't allowed more than a little foundation at school. To be honest I was glad it was banned as I wasn't all that bothered about wearing it. I figured a little here and there wouldn't hurt, and despite my reluctance to wear it daily, I was pretty good at applying it, thanks in part to the tutelage of my friend Lucy, who wore it more often when we met up outside of school.

I started with a very light coating of foundation, just to cover up some of those tiny pockmarks that the hotel mirror had conferred upon me. This was followed by a little eyeliner, a small amount of smoky grey eye shadow and a gentle brush of mascara on my eye lashes. I had no need for rouge as my rosy cheeks were still visible through my foundation and I figured

I would likely be blushing enough during the course of the evening.

I undid the towel from the top of my head and let my hair fall. It had dried very quickly and was naturally straight, largely because it was somewhat straw-like. I decided to hastily curl it around on top of my head and pin it into place. It was a technique my Mum had taught me once before when I had just washed it and we had to head out somewhere in a hurry. It was simple, yet elegant, and by wearing my hair up, as instructed, I would be revealing my neck, which I was assured was 'guaranteed' to get Mike to look at me differently.

Just as I had my hair in place with my hands and was about to grab a pin or two from my mouth, a knocking came from the door next to the wardrobe.

'5 minutes Becky.' came the instruction.

I tried to respond, but the combination of a mouth full of pins and my concentration in front of the mirror, led me to mumble something inaudible in the general direction of the door. Regardless, it was enough to make him walk away. I finished pinning up my hair and once I was happy with every last strand, I got up to put on the dress. I placed the dress on the floor and stepped into it, so as to not ruin my hair and make-up. I pulled it up over my hips and reached behind to do up the zip, a skill that every girl is taught from a young age and often requires very little dislocation of the shoulder.

I took a deep breath and dusted any marks or lint from the sides of the dress, straightening it around my waist as I did so. By this point, Mike was knocking from the corridor rather than the adjoining room. I walked over to the door, took one last look at myself in the full length bathroom mirror from the hallway, then turned and opened it. Mike was staring at the floor as usual, so I closed the door behind me, span round and stood firm, waiting for a reaction. Mike's eyes slowly raised from my heels, up my opaque black tights, past the hem of my dress, up to my pale chest and finally to my subtly made-up face and carefully styled hair.

'Wow,' said Mike, without a hint of awkwardness, 'you look so grown up.'

'Thanks.' I replied, before linking my arm through his and motioning towards the staircase.

As we walked through the reception area, towards the hotel restaurant, I beamed a smile at the women working on the front desk. I was almost dizzy with happiness – the whole scene felt somewhat surreal and the walk across the foyer seemed shorted than before. We reached the maître d' at the front of the restaurant and he showed us to a quiet, candle-lit corner table in the bustling dining room. I couldn't have chosen a more romantic location, I was convinced the staff must be aware of my quest. The waiter handed us two huge white menus, the size of which made it impossible to rest them on the table without risking setting fire to them on the candle, or dipping them in your water, preferably in that order.

I studied the menu intently. It was mainly French and Italian cuisine, written in their respective native tongues, which I – with my limited exposure to foreign languages at school – struggled to decipher. Luckily Mike was on hand to translate, although I suspected he was making approximations from cooking programmes he'd seen on daytime television since being out of work. I opted for the coq-au-vin, mainly for the thrill of hearing Mike say it, while he ordered a porterhouse steak that he hoped was at least as mouth-watering as it was eye-wateringly expensive.

'Can I get you anything to drink?' asked the waiter.

'Just a glass of house red with my steak, please.' said Mike.

The waiter's gaze shifted to my upturned wine glass and he began to lean over – I presumed – to take it away. Quick as a flash I reached out myself and turned it the right way up before filling it to the brim with iced water from the jug to my right. The waiter smiled, took our menus and backed away from the table.

As we had now relayed our order and the table was clear of cardboard fire hazards, I was able to relax slightly. As I did so I became aware of my toes pinching a little. I usually wore school socks with these shoes and even the relatively short walk from my room to the restaurant had caused me pain. I kicked them off under the table and plunged my stockinged toes deep into the thick carpet, tilting my head back momentarily as I did so. I let out a little sigh as my feet regained some feeling. I gazed over at Mike, through the flickering light of the candle and smiled. He smiled back, probably assuming I was excited about eating in a nice restaurant. I was of course, but I was far more excited about being seen out in public with him.

'So what's the plan for tomorrow?' I asked.

'Well, I thought we'd go and see a few of the famous sights, the Houses of Parliament, Big Ben, the Millennium Eye, then maybe the Tate Modern and St Paul's Cathedral. We don't have to go inside them all, but I thought you might like to at least see some of the places you'd otherwise only see on television!'

'Erm, yeah,' I responded, 'I guess that sounds ok. Will it take all day?'

'I think so yes, or at least most of the day.' said Mike.

It was at this moment that I realised that if I was going to get what I wanted from this trip, I might have to be a little more direct. I was trying to be amenable and amiable, but Mike didn't seem to realise that he and I might have different interests in terms of sight-seeing. I wanted to head to Oxford Street and go shopping in some of the famous department stores.

I relayed those thoughts to Mike and he quickly re-jigged his mental itinerary to make some time for shopping in the afternoon.

'Sorry, I guess I have a lot to learn about what teenage girls want eh?'

I smiled and nodded. The phrase "a lot to learn" had given me an increased sense of hope. Those specific words suggested to me that he might be in this for the long haul, that he wanted to learn and was willing to make the effort to please me. It didn't sound like the sort of thing he'd say if he was planning on dropping me back at my father's first thing on Monday morning.

I was still lost in thought when our food arrived. The waiter cleared his throat so I would move my elbow from between my knife and fork on the table. He set down the two plates and left us in peace to enjoy our meal.

I precisely picked my chicken from the bone, as daintily and as delicately as I could muster. It must have been hard for Mike to believe I was the same person who tore into that pizza the previous night. Mike on the other hand wrestled with his steak, tearing flesh from bone in an almost Neanderthal manner, stopping only to slurp some more red wine and rest his overworked wrists on occasion. It was actually hard for me to believe he was the same person who ate his pizza with a knife and fork.

We finished our meals at roughly the same time despite the relative size difference in our plates. I became conscious that we hadn't actually spoken to each other for the last ten minutes, absorbed as we were in quelling our appetites. We made idle small talk as Mike attempted to free gristle from his teeth with his tongue. The waiter cleared our plates and I persuaded Mike to split an ice cream sundae with me. They brought it out with two long spoons and we tucked in. Mike was careful to only take a few bites from one side, while I cherry-picked the best toppings, which were – rather aptly – cherries.

As Mike gave the waiter his room number to charge the meal to, I scanned the now almost empty dining room. We were a little late down for dinner, most tables were on their dessert when we arrived. The level of noise had quietened to almost none and the background hum of customers chattering was replaced by the occasional chinking of glassware behind the bar.

Mike looked over at me and started to get up from his seat. I automatically rose from mine and he offered his arm to me again. I put my hand just inside his elbow and we started walking slowly across the foyer. I don't know whether it was because I was tired, or because I was full, but I seemed to float across the dining room in a daydream-like state, until the calm was pierced by our waiter shouting after us.

'Excuse me Miss, excuse me... Miss?' he said, causing Mike and I to both turn around to look back and see what the problem was. The waiter was standing by our table with what appeared to be a pair of black shoes in his hand. Like a well-rehearsed double act Mike and I looked first at each other, then at our feet, spotting the tell-tale seam of a pair of tights across my toes. Mike laughed while I – on the other hand – turned a bright shade of pinkish-red in embarrassment.

I stood, rooted to the spot, in fear of looking any more stupid than I already did. This caused the waiter to stride the length of the restaurant and into the reception area with my shoes held aloft. With hindsight this was more embarrassing than if I'd walked back over to him in stockinged feet. He put them onto the floor next to me, as a parent would, which frankly was the worst thing he could have done. I smiled nervously and clung tightly onto Mike's arm as I attempted to slip them on without having to sit on the floor. Fortunately I was able to do so, averting a further crisis. I thanked the waiter and we headed back across the reception area. This time I didn't smile at the women on the desk, but they smiled at me. Unfortunately it was the sort of patronising smile one gives to a child when they've done something cute – like forget to put their shoes on.

As we walked up the stairs and through the corridor towards our rooms, Mike reminded me that we had an early start for sightseeing tomorrow and warned me to not stay up too late. After my latest embarrassing set-back I just wanted to curl up in bed anyway. Tomorrow was another day and should provide a better opportunity for me to get close to Mike – without the driver and passenger dynamic mirroring that of parent and child.

Once I'd said goodnight and headed into my room I couldn't wait to kick my shoes off and get out of my tights. My poor toes looked squashed and a little red, so I sat on the bed and fanned my toes out, allowing the fresh air to soothe them. I removed my make-up gently with a cleansing wipe, before carefully pulling my dress over my head. I extricated myself from my padded bra and threw my usual sleep t-shirt on before cleaning my teeth and getting into bed.

I tucked myself tightly into the large king-sized bed – the sheets were soft and the pillows were just the right level of firmness. The feel of brand new bed linen was one of life's simplest pleasures. I always enjoyed my first night in clean sheets at home, although my father changed them less often than my mum had. I fully intended to have an early night – as I'd promised Mike – but I couldn't resist picking up the magazine again and quickly flicking to step two of 'Five steps to snag your man'.

"Step two: Talk about *him*.

Guys love nothing more than talking about themselves, so make sure you give him the opportunity. When talking about yourself, think about how to make your life seem more interesting. Be sure to ask questions about him and be attentive, really listen to his answers, nod and smile to show him you're interested in his responses."

I realised I hadn't really had a proper conversation with Mike. I thought I knew a reasonable amount about him already, but in a way he didn't seem to like to talk about himself much. Or maybe he did but just never had the opportunity. I would have to steer our dialogue in that direction in order to find out. I would have liked to know more about him anyway and I was sure I wouldn't have to feign interest in the answers he gave to my questions. I closed up the magazine and played out an imaginary conversation in my head as I dozed off.

Chapter 6

Mike woke me early for breakfast and I was still a little sleepy by the time I was back up in my room afterwards, getting changed into something suitable for the day. I peered out of the window, the pavement below was bathed in sunlight. I opted for my Capri pants and a vest top, then put on my sandals and popped my sunglasses on top of my head and made my way out to meet Mike who was already waiting for me in the corridor. He stood in a pair of chinos and a polo shirt. It was a slightly brighter polo shirt than yesterday. '*Clearly from his summer collection.*' I thought.

'Ready to go?' said Mike in a voice much too cheery for that time of morning.

I grunted something indecipherable in response and we walked side by side down the staircase, through reception and out of the large revolving door onto the street. The first thing that hit me as we left the hotel was the heat, not just in the direct sunlight, but the oppressive humidity of a bustling metropolis. I was used to sunny days at home but they were always accompanied by a stiff sea breeze – the heat here was stifling and took my breath away.

We walked a short distance down the street to the nearest tube station. I anticipated blessed relief from the heat as we ducked inside a dark tunnel, but I was mistaken. Inside the tube station rushes of hot air made their way up escalator shafts and poured out into the street above. The air felt dirty, like walking too close to the back of a bus as it pulls away.

Mike had picked up a couple of travel cards at the hotel before breakfast and instructed me to simply tap it on the gate and walk through. I duly did so, before walking into an immobile barrier, causing a few regular tube users to titter at my misfortune. '*Way to start the day, Becky.*' I thought, before catching Mike doing exactly the same thing seconds later beside me. It turned out we were at the exit barriers, once we'd recalibrated our entry point we stood atop a giant escalator, three of four times larger than any I'd seen before. Mike stood on the right hand side and marshalled me in behind him.

Nobody talked in tube stations, aside from broken English at the ticket office. The escalators were silent, save for the sound of the trains and the air displacement below. As I stood on the step behind Mike and the escalator began its descent I realised I was now around the same height as him. I paused and reflected on this fact for a moment. It was nice to feel his equal, even if just for a short time.

Inexplicably, I found myself leaning forward slightly towards him. My nose was at the height of the freshly shorn hairs at the top of his neck, my mouth in line with his collar. I closed my eyes and leaned in further, as if about to kiss the back of his neck. I breathed in deeply through my nose and as I opened one eye slightly, I saw his neck raise up in front of me, closer to my eye level. I leant back slightly, initially confused, before realising this could mean only one thing.

I stumbled slightly as the tips of my sandals reached the static floor below the escalator. I was aware enough of my surroundings to 'style it out' and make it look like I simply had a skip in my step as I brought myself back alongside Mike. I looked up at him and smiled and counted my blessings that I'd snapped myself out of that daydream just in time. I didn't want our first kiss to be one he was unaware of, especially not if it was followed by me bundling him to the dusty floor of the tube station.

We walked over to a congested platform and waited for the next train. The electronic screen above showed three trains arriving in the next six minutes, all going in the same direction. I was used to waiting *sixty* minutes for a bus back home. As we waited I stuck close to Mike and looked around at the other passengers – a mix of day-trippers, foreign tourists and the odd workaholic who seemed to be heading to the office on a Saturday. I noticed a woman a few feet away who was looking over in our direction. Initially I thought she was just people-watching as I was, but she stared a little too long at Mike for my liking.

I inched closer to my travel companion and made a grab for his hand just as the sign above said train approaching. He gripped my hand tightly, assuming I was nervous about fighting my way onto the crowded train. I turned back to look at the woman, smiled knowingly at her and prepared to board the train. It was at this point that I realised I could utilise the dad and daughter relationship when it suited me, and shun it when it didn't. I had the inside track, home advantage, I could legitimately hold his hand and ward off other potential suitors without reproach. I smiled to myself and let Mike guide me onto the busy train carriage.

We were only due to be on the tube for a few minutes, which was just as well as the heat on the crowded train was almost unbearable. We stood at one end of the carriage, by a window of sorts, but the breeze wasn't cool and I could feel beads of sweat forming around the hairs on the back of my neck.

Our first stop was to be Westminster, home to the houses of parliament, the seat of government of the United Kingdom and a worldwide symbol of democracy. Or so Mike told me, to me it was the building on the brown sauce bottle and the clock that bonged on New Year's Eve. In fact, as we made our way out of Westminster station, which was, on the whole, a lot cleaner and nicer than the station we'd got on at, the clock made the very sound I was familiar with. Mike informed me that Big Ben bonged every hour and the number of bongs after the tune correlated to the time. I felt a little silly for not realising that and decided that the occasional cultural lesson might actually be beneficial.

We made our way across the road and stood in front of the imposing building. Mike had brought his camera and was keen to get some good photographs. As he leant further and further back to get everything in shot he realised he had been better off over the road by the tube station. He duly crossed back over to finish snapping away. I walked the short distance to a small green area on the corner of the parliament buildings, and sat on the grass. Mike peeled his eye away from the viewfinder and looked across the road.

I could see his head twitch to and fro and his eyes dart from side to side as he tried to figure out where I was. I could see him from where I sat, and thus he could see me too, but I wasn't about to wave or shout or do anything embarrassing. Instead, I sat and waited until he caught sight of me and came rushing over.

I sat with my arms locked straight behind me and my palms pressed firmly into the warm grass. I'd kicked off my sandals and ran my toes through what remained of the early morning dew. I had my sunglasses on but I still needed to squint as I looked up at Mike who was now bearing down on me. I smiled, in order to let him know that everything was ok and he needn't worry. As I did so I sensed the lecture he'd prepared for me on the dangers of wandering off in the big city.

'Sorry, I just didn't want to stand by the road getting covered in exhaust fumes when there was this nice little park over here.' I said pre-emptively.

Mike said nothing, smiled, and sat down next to me on the grass.

We sat for around ten minutes, enjoying the sunshine on our skin, watching the people and the cars rushing by. We were delaying other items on our itinerary but neither of us wanted to be the one to interrupt such a pleasant moment by clock-watching.

I couldn't believe the frantic pace of London. I sat the same way in parks at home, but here it felt like I was on a calm island in the middle of chaos, or as if I were watching London on a huge wrap-around 3D television. I didn't feel part of it and it certainly seemed to carry on functioning regardless of my observing it.

I began to feel a new sensation on my skin, transcending from warm and sun-kissed towards sunburnt. I stood up just in time to catch a breeze making its way through the trees on the park perimeter and it cooled me sufficiently to ease my discomfort. I looked down at Mike who consulted me on whether it was time to move on, before standing up and motioning in the direction of Westminster Bridge.

We walked once again past the 'brown sauce building', before heading over the bridge. As we crossed the river we stopped to watch a couple of boats pass underneath. The Thames was a hive of activity in the summer, tourist boats, the river police, even a public transport route running down the river, stopping at various landmarks along the way. All we saw was a small nondescript boat and some flotsam, or possibly jetsam, I wasn't sure of the difference. The river was a dark grey colour, even on a bright sunny day like this it seemed to suck the life out of the landscape. We decided it wasn't that nice to look at after all and moved on to the South Bank.

To our left we could see the London Eye, a monstrous 'big wheel' built as part of the millennium celebrations and left to dominate the skyline on the south of the river. It looked strangely out of place amongst both the old buildings of Parliament Square and the newer skyscrapers of the City of London behind it. As we approached the embarking point the crowds were horrendous. A line of people snaked in front, while many more just stood and contemplated joining them. We didn't deliberate for long, deciding to stand on the grass in the shadow of the wheel and watch it go round. It was much slower than I'd imagined and it stopped every few minutes to let people on and off. It seemed less like a must-see tourist attraction, more a claustrophobe's nightmare.

We intended to watch it make one complete revolution, but after ten minutes the pod had only made it through two or three positions and we gave up and started walking east down the riverbank. We passed Royal Festival Hall and The Royal National Theatre, huge concrete monstrosities the architectural zeitgeist had not been kind to.

My enthusiasm for the day was beginning to wane a little as Mike took endless pictures of these vast, grey, post-war buildings. He then spotted another up ahead, the OXO tower he told me, though that was plainly clear from the huge letters spelling it out down the side. We walked a few hundred yards further to get a better angle to photograph it, unintentionally stumbling across a sign to 'Gabriel's Wharf' which piqued my interest much more.

'Can I go and have a look down here while you're taking photos?' I asked, aware that I shouldn't run off unseen again.

'Sure' said Mike, 'I'll meet you in there in a bit, just don't go too far.'

I walked through the iron gates and to my amazement the path opened up into a quaint little square of arty looking shops and cafés, a little haven from the functional concrete buildings of the South Bank, complete with flowers and plants in hanging baskets, brightly coloured shop fronts and eclectic music emanating from behind every door.

I walked into the first shop on my right, a cornucopia of brightly-coloured clothes greeted me, as well as a girl a few years older than me with pierced nose and eyebrows. I felt a little dizzy at first, my visual cortex overloaded by the swirling patterns, but I eventually grew accustomed to it and began studying the dresses more carefully. I found one I particularly liked and was holding it against myself when the pierced girl crept up behind me.

'Hey, that dress would look beautiful on you, ya know?'

I spun round and beamed a little.

'Thanks, it's really pretty.' I replied.

'There's changing rooms at the back there if you want to try it on.'

I paused for a moment, considering that Mike might not find me if I was in a changing room.

'Go on, you owe it to yourself to at least try it on!' insisted the girl with the piercings.

I agreed and headed to the back of the store, despite the fact that I had no money to buy the dress.

As I got to the back of the ramshackle shop, I realised the changing room was nothing more than a few poles erected 5 feet or so apart with curtains attached to them. Nevertheless I stepped inside and attempted to close the curtain behind me. I pulled and pulled but the stiff folds of the fabric seemed to stop the curtain short of the pole at the end, leaving a gap of an inch or so. I took a deep breath and started to undress, discarding my clothes in the corner.

As I was stood in my underwear I glanced quickly through the small gap in the curtain and saw a man about Mike's height on the far side of the shop. As he turned round I quickly realised it wasn't in fact Mike, so I hurriedly grabbed the dress and held it against me again. I sheepishly moved over to one corner of my little booth – where I felt less exposed – before putting on the floral print dress.

As I stood in front of the mirror inside the changing room I flicked the corner of the dress back and forth, simulating it swaying in the breeze. I felt great wearing it, it looked every bit as pretty on me as it had on the hanger, which is a rare occurrence for a girl when out clothes shopping. I took a peek out of the gap in the curtain to look for the pierced girl, hoping I could glean another compliment from her. To my surprise, she was now standing by the tills talking to Mike.

I stepped out of the booth, leaving my clothes in the corner, to signal to either of them that I was here. The pierced girl pointed over to me and Mike wandered over, with her following a few yards behind, smelling a sale. No sooner had Mike arrived at the changing rooms than the pierced girl stepped up her patter.

'Doesn't she look beautiful?' she said in Mike's direction.

Mike now found himself in a slightly awkward situation. The default position of a dad, when referring to his daughter, is that she is indeed the most beautiful girl in the world. For him to say that about me however, was – I suspected – a little more complicated. This made his response all the more flattering.

'She really does.' said Mike.

'Would you like to take that one then?' the pierced girl asked him.

'What do you think Becky? Would you like it?' said Mike, shifting his gaze from her to me.

'I... erm... well, yes.' I said, still rather taken aback by the course of events.

'Then we'll take it.' said Mike to the pierced girl, who smiled at him and then me in turn.

I skipped the few paces over to where Mike was standing and wrapped my arms around him. I pressed my cheek into his chest and squeezed him firmly, before skipping back into the changing room to change out of the dress. I pulled the curtain back across to its previous position, an inch or so from the end of the pole.

Mike stepped up to the curtain and stood with his back to me, in front of the gap, facing out into the shop. I felt much more comfortable changing this time, so much so that as I stood in my underwear, bent at the waist, to pick up my clothes from the corner, I suddenly remembered how Mike had – inadvertently or otherwise – looked at my bum in the rear view mirror. '*If he turned around now he'd get an even better view!*' I thought, before standing back up and finishing getting dressed.

I peeled back the curtain – which startled Mike slightly – and stepped out of the booth.

'Are you sure this is ok?' I asked, 'I only tried it on cos the girl said it would look nice on me. I wasn't expecting you to find me in this shop so quickly.'

'Of course it's okay. If a dad can't buy his daughter a dress...' said Mike, before I cut him off.

'Uhuh, but... well, you know?' I said, suggesting he drop the charade for a moment.

'It's fine. It's not expensive and you looked so happy wearing it.' said Mike.

'Thanks.' I said. I was thanking him for buying the dress, but also for recognising when I was happy and trying to foster that emotion in me.

Mike paid with his credit card and passed me the bag, I hooked it over my left arm and linked my right through his as we walked out the shop. I turned to look at the pierced girl who was smiling back at me. She knew – as I did – just how lucky I was to have him.

We sauntered around the rest of the little shops, showcasing seashell-surround mirrors and driftwood cheese boards, as well as clocks made from old vinyl records. I kept my arm linked through Mike's for as long as was practical, picking up interesting objects with my left hand, before realising I wasn't as ambidextrous as I thought I might be. Eventually I gave up and relinquished my hold on him for the sake of fingering some key rings.

'Are we done here?' asked Mike, glancing at his watch and with a tone of voice that suggested we most definitely were.

'Yeah ok, where are we off to next?' I asked.

'Well I could do with taking the weight off my feet for a bit, there's a nice pub overlooking the Thames a bit further up. Maybe we could stop there and get something small for lunch?' he said.

'Sounds good to me.' I replied, excited at the prospect of being invited to the pub for the first time.

Chapter 7

As we walked back towards the riverbank some clouds passed overhead and the light dimmed instantaneously in a way that my eyes struggled to adjust to at quite the same speed. I bumped straight into the side of Mike as he stopped to take off his sunglasses. I used this opportunity to do the same and slid mine back up onto the top of my head. The river looked even greyer now, reflecting as it would, the dark clouds above. It wasn't long before we reached the pub Mike had mentioned. We were glad to get out of the muggy warm air.

Mike walked straight up to the bar. I followed sheepishly, a few paces behind. The pub was quite busy and there was a constant low-level hum of conversation, only the odd word here and there was audible and could come from any one of a number of different sources. I stood behind Mike as he grabbed the barman's attention by waving his hand like he was hailing a cab.

'Hi, can I get a pint of Bishop's Mitre, a coke and do you have any menus?'

'You got any ID mate?' came the barman's response.

Mike – looking a little confused as he probably hadn't been asked for ID in a pub for many years – questioned what the barman had said.

'ID?'

'Yeah, ID,' he reiterated, 'for the girl. There's no kids allowed in the pub, sorry.'

Mike looked round at me, standing patiently behind him and saying nothing.

'It's my daughter, she's over sixteen, she's not a crying toddler. We'll only sit in a corner somewhere and have a quick lunch and be gone, nobody's gonna mind surely?' said Mike, his voice raised somewhat.

'Sorry mate, if she can't drink, she can't be in here.' came the barman's response.

Mike turned to look at me again. This time I remained silent but motioned my head in the direction of the door to suggest we go elsewhere. People were starting to stare, Mike's protestations had drawn a bit of an audience and the hum of conversation now seemed to include references to me. What seemed at first a friendly environment felt a little more hostile and I didn't really want to stay even if they relented. Mike's annoyance at the situation only added to this feeling. I didn't want to prevent him from having his pint. I may as well have been that screaming toddler, I was having the same effect on him.

'Sorry, Becky.' said Mike with a look of resignation etched across his face. 'Let's go find a cafe or something to sit and grab some food in.'

I nodded and turned to leave the pub, this time with Mike walking a few paces behind *me*.

The experience in the pub felt like another blow to my hopes of changing our relationship. If I was going to be successful in making Mike think of me as an equal – a potential partner – I had to stop getting into 'parent and child' situations. Anything with an age requirement was out, cinema, pubs and bars, even tourist attractions with adult and child pricing. If Mike suggested any of those things I'd simply say I wasn't interested, that way we could plan activities that would stop the trivial issue of my age coming up again.

In the meantime, as we walked a little further along the riverbank, I thought to myself that it was interesting how easy it was for Mike to lie about my age. He had told the barman I was over sixteen, without batting an eyelid. I liked that he was able to do that, to lie for me in that way. If he was prepared to lie to someone else about my age, perhaps he was prepared to lie to himself too.

We passed the OXO tower, found a little cafe next door and headed inside for some food. Mike stood staring at the selection of sandwiches and salads on offer for some time. I think he was frantically searching for something reminiscent of the pub grub he was so looking forward to. He settled on an all-day breakfast baguette, despite the fact we'd already had breakfast at... well... breakfast-time. I plumped for a pesto chicken salad and a little pot of fruit, sliced and packaged in a way that makes it so much more appetising than regular whole pieces of fruit. Mike ordered a black coffee, seemingly still pining for his pint of stout. I pointed to some kind of fruit flavoured iced coffee drink on the wall behind the cashier.

We sat at the quietest corner we could, which was still comparatively noisy, while the bright fluorescent light assaulted our eyes. We'd traded a dimly lit, cosy pub, for a bright, airy, fast food style coffee establishment and it provided no respite for us. I decided to cheer Mike up with a suggestion.

'Hey, sorry we couldn't get lunch in the pub today but I've got a suggestion.

Mike looked up at me from his cold and limp baguette, forcing a smile as he asked what it was. He didn't seem convinced that I could actually come up with a good idea.

'Well, I noticed they had a 'traditional' selection on the room service menu in our hotel – Toad in the Hole, Lasagne, Sausages and Mash, that sort of thing. Why don't we get some beers from a supermarket near the hotel and turn our two rooms into our very own spacious pub, complete with pub grub?'

'Now that *is* a good idea.' said Mike enthusiastically. 'We'll be tired from traipsing around London all day, so we probably won't feel like going out again anyway.'

'I told you it was a good idea.'

'Thanks Rebecca.' said Mike, with a more considered smile on his face this time.

I held a piece of pesto-drenched chicken from my salad in front of my mouth, deep in thought. Mike rarely called me that, in fact nobody called me that. The last person to call me Rebecca was my mother.

That wasn't the reason I was stopped in my tracks by it though, that was more to do with the fact that it seemed so grown up when *he* said it. Sure I liked when he called me Princess, but that was a dad and daughter kind of thing. I even liked it when he called me Becky, like we were friends, which I'd always considered we were. When he called me Rebecca, however, I felt like a peer, or better still, his partner. I said it over and over in my head 'Mike and Rebecca', 'Mike and Rebecca'. I imagined someone introducing us at a party, 'Oh that's Mike and Rebecca'.

I suddenly realised I was staring off into middle distance and quickly pushed the fork into my mouth. The fork was empty, however, the piece of chicken having fallen off at some point during my daydream. I bit down on the tines in my dreamlike state and it made an awful clanging sound. I coughed audibly to throw my companion off the scent and picked up the piece of chicken again. Mike was too busy looking at his limp baguette to notice, although now he seemed to be smiling and deep in thought himself. It was nice to see him smile.

We finished our snacks and coffees and as we looked outside the sky appeared to have brightened a little. The next stop on our walking tour of London was to be the Tate Modern, an art gallery situated in a converted power station. We made the short walk down the south bank towards the imposing brick structure. A large chimney, a remnant of the building's former use, towered over the site and was the first thing we spotted on our approach. I'd never been to an art gallery of any kind before, modern or otherwise, so entering the vast open space of the turbine hall was a slightly surreal experience, particularly as at that point I couldn't see anything I could identify as art.

'Amazing building, isn't it?' said Mike, appearing to allow the majesty of the empty space to wash over him.

'Erm... yeah.' I responded, feeling altogether less at ease with how insignificant I felt inside it.

It was eerily quiet inside the vast empty hall which presumably was once filled with the rumble of generators. The silence was soon interrupted by a large party coming through the sliding entrance doors behind us. Their conversation echoed around the empty chamber and created a cacophony of sound that steadily increased in volume and complexity. My relationship with the vacuous space shifted from one of isolation to one of chaotic inclusion. It was then that I felt I understood the meaning of this grandiose yet sparse entrance hall, it highlighted perfectly the link between sensory stimulus and psychological interpretation.

I stepped a little closer to Mike, but stopped short of linking arms with him again, as we walked side by side down the sloped floor towards a set of doors off to the left. As we arrived there it became obvious that the side of the building overlooking the Thames was where the exhibition and gallery spaces were. We headed down a narrow corridor to the first square room with white-washed walls punctuated only by brightly coloured canvases and small placards denoting the artist and title of each work.

'Can you explain things to me as we go along?' I asked. 'Like what they mean.'

Mike smiled, presumably nervous at the notion that he should provide insight into such abstract works of art that even critics and artists themselves could not agree upon the meaning thereof.

'It's really all about interpretation.' Mike eventually replied. 'You're supposed to take what you want from each piece. Whatever it means to you, that's what it means.'

I didn't really understand what his response meant, let alone what the paintings meant.

I allowed myself to wander around the room, stopping at paintings that commanded I do so. I darted between canvases in a seemingly random fashion, much to the annoyance of other visitors, who preferred to move from one to the other in either a clockwise or anti-clockwise pattern – as if the viewing of abstract art required some structure in order to make it more palatable. Once I'd shrugged off the burden of understanding, or interpretation, I found the paintings a lot more interesting. So much so, that I'd quickly devoured one room and was heading into the next when I heard Mike call out to me to wait, in case he lost me again. I told him I'd never go more than one room ahead, he accepted this premise and allowed me to continue roaming.

The next room had less abstract works on display. I came across a painting which intrigued me and caused me to stop and stare at it for longer than I had most of the others thus far. It was entitled 'Morning' and the artist was listed as 'Dod Procter'. The placard only gave me slightly more information, it was painted in 1926, the model's name was Cissie Barnes and she was sixteen years old when she sat for the artist.

Despite our similar ages, Cissie and I were, in many ways, remarkably dissimilar. Cissie was much fuller figured, as her bedsheets wrapped around her they produced pleasing contours, her shapely breasts protruded proudly through her nightgown. '*If I lay flat on my back*' – I thought – '*my sheets would cling to me tightly and produce almost no deviation in the shape of the cloth*'.

Cissie had dirt under her nails and red marks on her arms and around her knuckles, she looked like she had done more than a few days of physical labour, despite her relatively young age. She lay on the bed, eyes closed, with a tranquil look upon her face. I hoped that I too looked that picturesque first thing in the morning. I imagined the vantage point of the artist painting this picture, from around three or four feet away I calculated, standing up and looking down on young Cissie. I couldn't help but envisage Mike standing over me in that way.

I closed my eyes and allowed myself to embellish the daydream with more detail. As I did so, I swore I could feel Mike's hand on my shoulder as I lay there. Of course the sensation was made all the more real by the fact he *actually* had his hand on my shoulder as I stood in front of the painting. Only when I opened my eyes and turned my head did I notice the change in pressure as he removed his hand and spoke.

'Hey, sorry, didn't mean to sneak up on you, just wanted to let you know I was here.' said Mike.

'It's ok, I was just lost in this painting.' I replied.

'I'm gonna head into the next room, but you can stay here if you like – just catch up with me.'

'No it's ok, I'm done here. I'd like to walk around with you if that's ok?' I said.

'Of course.' said Mike, happy that I'd returned to the realm of the living and communicative.

We linked arms once again and made our way into the next room. I struggled to banish from my mind the image of Mike standing over me whilst I lay in bed. Worse still, it was now 'Shower Mike' in my vision, which made it even more difficult to shake. I decided to remain quiet and allow those feelings to wash over me, hoping they would eventually be quelled but somehow knowing that – like the tides – they would be unrelenting.

Before I knew it, we'd visited six more rooms and were heading back out of the gallery space altogether. I guess Mike had assumed that I had lost interest and was a little bored by now, as I hadn't stopped at any of the paintings for any length of time. Truth was, I was barely aware of my surroundings. I'd only avoided walking into walls and door frames thanks to the guiding arm of my companion. For the last forty-five minutes I wasn't Becky, or even Rebecca. I was Cissie, reclining on a bed with sheets barely covering my body. How I longed for Mike to see me like that. I didn't know what he'd think upon stumbling across such a scene, but I felt sure he'd be compelled to stop and stare for at least a moment.

'Shall we make a move?' asked Mike.

'Yeah ok, sorry, I was miles away.' I explained.

'Tell you what, I think we've done enough cultural stuff for now, why don't we head to Oxford Street and have a look round some of the shops this afternoon?'.

'Is that where the big department stores are?' I asked eagerly.

'Yeah a short walk up from there, but there's lots of other shops, I don't mind you dragging me around them for a while.'

I smiled at the thought of getting to go shopping in London, but also at the notion of me dragging Mike around anywhere. Physically it would of course be impossible, but figuratively I was more than happy to give it a go.

Chapter 8

We headed over the Millennium Bridge – just outside the art gallery – in the direction of the bright blue-green dome of St Paul's Cathedral, which towered above the rest of the skyline, except for the cranes. Mike stopped a couple of times to take pictures along the way, both of the Thames and St Paul's. The bridge was crowded and it made walking on it rather surreal. It swayed a little as we did so and I recalled seeing on the news that when initially opened it swayed a little too much for most tourists liking. I quite enjoyed the feeling, it made me feel a part of something larger, a movement, a migration, like a herd of wildebeest on the plains of Africa.

We reached the other side, away from the watering holes of the south bank and nearer the City of London and the Bank of England, at which – as Mike told me – I was not allowed to open an account. I was mildly disappointed not to be heading back to school next term with a Bank of England debit card. That would have shown Brooke who came in every day with her dad's credit card. We were aiming for St Paul's tube station, which was just behind the cathedral. I did insist though, that Mike stop to take all the pictures he wanted, while we were there.

I sat, once again, on a small patch of grass, and kicked off my sandals. This time I looked up at the sky, full of fluffy white clouds which disappointingly didn't form any discernible shapes of interest. How people spot faces or the outlines of objects in the clouds I'll never know. It reminded me of the Rorschach ink-blot test. I always felt that to agree to participate in the test was a sure sign of at least several of the psychological disorders it was intended to diagnose. I stared at the voluminous abstract objects for a few minutes until once again I felt a hand on my shoulder. This time I jumped both figuratively and literally.

'Jeez, you're gonna have to stop doing that.' I said, my voice still trembling slightly.

'Sorry Miss,' said a distinctly deep voice with an American twang, 'I was gonna ask if you wouldn't mind taking a picture for us?'

I looked up and over my shoulder to see a set of strange faces looking back at me. A portly chap in a wind cheater and shorts, an equally portly woman in a remarkably similar outfit, and three altogether slimmer girls, about my age, all dressed in the same shorts and styles of jacket, with only varying colours to tell them apart. It was like something out of a horror movie, I frantically scanned the horizon for Mike in the hope that he could save me from this awkward situation. Alas he was busy with his eye to the viewfinder and seemed less concerned with my whereabouts with every passing stop on our trip.

'Er, sure.' I said, standing up and brushing the loose grass from the backs of my legs.

The portly chap handed me a camera, insisting on putting the strap around my neck, which made me rather uncomfortable. Once I looked at the device it became clear to me why he had defied social convention to keep his camera safe. It was enormous, jam packed with buttons on every available surface and with a grid over the screen with which to line up the family and the cathedral with the horizon.

'You should be able to just point and shoot Miss, I've already zoomed in to the required level.' he said.

It felt strange being called Miss. I wasn't sure anybody had ever called me it before, it was usually the term I used to greet female teachers at my school. It was certainly polite though, presumably in deference to my being a native of this country. He wasn't to know I was a mere impostor in this city.

I lined up the shot, but despite the zoom level apparently being correct, I was still cutting off half of the blue-jacketed girl from the picture. Rather than attempt to figure out which of the many buttons would zoom out fractionally I opted to try and get her slightly closer to the purple-jacketed girl.

'Erm, sorry, can the girl in the blue jacket just squeeze in a little more?' I asked.

'MEG, GET CLOSER TO JENNY!' bellowed the man, causing everyone to stand closer to each other, as well as more upright and attentive.

If anything I now had too much extra room in the shot, but I wasn't about to say so.

I pressed the shutter and took, what I thought, was a lovely photograph of a gaggle of Americans in front of St Paul's Cathedral.

'Right, everyone stay where you are.' said the portly man, in a slightly lower tone of voice than before, but still significantly louder than anyone else in the immediate vicinity. I too remained rooted to the spot just in case.

He walked over and asked to take a look at the photograph, not waiting for me to remove the strap from my neck he leant in next to me and pressed a button to allow him to view the last shot. By now he was standing very close to me – he smelt faintly of fried onions.

'Ah that's great Miss, thanks very much for your time.' he said, breathing more onion fumes into the side of my face, warming my cheek as he did so.

He removed the camera strap once again from my neck, his fingers brushing past my hair as he did so, before reaching into his pocket and grabbing a scrap of paper.

'Here, this is for you.' he said, handing me the crumpled piece of paper and turning back to his family, who were already making their way into the cathedral.

At that moment Mike appeared to my right with a concerned look on his face. All he had seen from his vantage point, was the portly man with his arms around my neck, before leaving me standing looking slightly confused, smelling faintly of onions, with a crumpled five pound note in my left hand.

'What was that for?' asked Mike.

I looked down at the crumpled note in my hand, it had only just struck me what it was.

'Oh, he just wanted to take a picture... erm... wanted me to take a picture.' I replied.

I didn't really understand why he'd paid me five pounds to do so, he certainly hadn't mentioned that when we'd entered into the agreement. It seemed to me like more than a fair reward for two minutes work, although with hindsight it only recompensed the anxiety I felt having him stand so close to me.

I tucked the five pound note into my right hand pants pocket and smiled, to let Mike know everything was ok.

'At least now I have some spending money for the shops.'

Mike smiled back awkwardly. I liked that he was a little overprotective of me, I didn't consider it parental protectiveness, despite the fact he was clearly a guardian in my father's absence. I preferred to think of it as him wanting me all to himself, that when another man got close to me his reaction was, first and foremost, one of jealousy.

We headed for St Paul's underground station and minutes later were back on a crowded and sweaty tube train heading west towards Oxford Circus. The smell of onions that had transferred from the American man to myself now began to permeate through the tube carriage. I suspected that his hands, when brushing my neck and hair, had been the culprit in passing his scent on to me. I was beginning to feel that the five pounds he'd paid me wasn't enough.

We arrived at Oxford Circus station and as I prepared myself for squeezing past people to disembark, I soon realised we weren't the only ones getting off at this stop. I also had to contend with people trying to get on the tube train, laden with brightly coloured shopping bags, the thick paper kind that keep their shape and create a fan-like effect when stacked against the thigh. As luck would have it the guy in front of me admonished all the would-be passengers, reminding them to let us off the train first. As a result my route off the train was much easier than I'd initially anticipated.

Mike on the other hand was trying, inexplicably, to get off at another set of doors, further proving my theory that the longer this day went on, the less concerned he was for my whereabouts. I stepped over to one side of the platform and waited for him to find me, which he eventually did. We made our way up the escalators, through the barriers and out onto street level. We were instantly greeted by the sight of what seemed like half the population of the UK, spread equally across the four corners of the busy junction, all waiting for the lights to change, so that they might transpose themselves into shops on the opposite side of the road.

This time, Mike insisted I stay close to him. I wasn't about to argue, I could see myself getting lost in minutes amongst these crowds. We stopped on the corner and surveyed our immediate surroundings. I could see a large clothes shop over the road and wanted to make that our first destination. Mike suggested we walk down Regent St first, to visit the toy shop. I didn't really want to, but he insisted it was a 'must-see' and I didn't want to disappoint him. We meandered in the general direction of the toy shop, as one must do when walking on the busy streets of London, until ten minutes later we'd finally beaten a path to its door.

I had to hand it to Mike, it was a pretty impressive sight. The shop was enormous, spread across six floors, but more thrilling was that everywhere you looked there were staff demonstrating products and interacting with the kids. It was like the toy stores I'd seen in Christmas movies but assumed weren't real.

We wandered around aimlessly for a short while. I wasn't about to pick up some soft toys with Mike around, however much I wanted to on occasion. Instead I enjoyed looking at the children tugging their parent's sleeves and their eyes lighting up every time an adult reached into their pocket or handbag for a wallet or purse.

Mike wandered over to a section of cheap 'pocket money' toys and had soon stumbled across a variety of plastic treats he recognised from his childhood. His eyes lit up, just like the children I'd seen minutes earlier, as he waved me over to lecture me on how much better toys were in the old days.

'Look, we called these poppers, have you ever seen these before'? He said, turning a small rubber half-sphere upside down and waiting patiently for it to leap into the air.

'Yeah, we had those in primary school years ago, as a craze they only lasted for about six months before a kid got one in his eye and ruined it for the rest of us.' I replied, just as the 'popper' popped sideways into the air and struck a passer-by.

Mike and I grinned at each other and then let our eyes wander elsewhere so as to appear inconspicuous. I reached for a yo-yo in the next box and attempted to successfully release and retrieve it. I had got quite good with a yo-yo at primary school, when they'd made their last comeback. The new ones were precision modelled plastic, with machined and oiled ball bearings, much better for doing tricks with. Mike was stunned by my prowess and the way I could manipulate it upwards with the merest flick of my finger.

'I bet you still had the old wooden ones back in your day eh?' I asked cheekily.

'Yeah, that's right, one step up from the hoop and stick!' replied Mike, sarcastically.

I had no idea what the hoop and stick was, but at that moment I sensed my joke had backfired on both of us slightly.

'Oh wow, clackers, do you remember these?' said Mike enthusiastically, picking up some more brightly coloured plastic.

'I can't say I do, no.' I replied, confused by how what he had in his hand could constitute a toy.

Mike then proceeded to swing the plastic toy up and down, gently at first, making two plastic balls bash into each other. His swinging slowly gathered pace, which resulted in the deafening clang of plastic on plastic over and over again. By now, everyone around us had stopped to look at who, or what, was causing the infernal racket. He self-consciously grabbed the clackers with his free hand to quieten them before returning them to the box.

I suggested it might be time to leave, as once again we had garnered more attention than we would have liked. Our audible conversation about poppers, clackers and yo-yo's must have sounded more like we were dealing recreational drugs rather than reminiscing over recreational toys. Either way, I was itching to go to the clothes shop I'd seen from the junction. Mike could sense he was fighting a losing battle and succumbed to letting me head back to Oxford St and my date with shopping destiny.

We arrived to be greeted by thumping music and two staff members directing the pedestrian traffic.

'Girls downstairs, Guys upstairs.' said one, as we stopped in our tracks and blocked the doorway.

'I'll go and have a wander upstairs then and come down and find you in a bit.' said Mike loudly over the music.

I decided not to shout back and just nodded in his direction before heading to the nearest escalator. I made my way down to the basement floor and felt instantly at home amongst the throngs of teenagers, either on their own or in small groups, heads down, flicking through racks of clothing, or giggling and chatting to each other. I spotted some t-shirts I liked and walked over to have a closer look. I overheard a conversation between two girls on the other side of the display I was standing at.

'Yeah, but I like older guys, so I don't think I would go out with Liam anyway.' said the first voice.

'I know, but he's cute and you know he likes you, so what if he's the same age as us?' said the second.

'But Darren was nineteen and had a job and everything. Liam won't be able to take me places.'

I chuckled a little to myself at what I was hearing. I hardly thought nineteen qualified someone as an older guy in that context. As I did so I suddenly became aware that the dividing wall between myself and the girls on the other side was Perspex and I could feel two sets of eyes attempting to burn a hole in it. I quickly turned on my heels and decided to investigate another corner of the basement signposted 'vintage clothing'.

I wasn't long flicking through this second display when I realised I perhaps didn't enjoy clothes shopping as much as I had thought I did. Every time I found something I liked I saw someone else wander over and pick it up, this made me realise that before long we'd all be walking around in the same outfits if we weren't careful. I clutched the bag in my hand with the dress I'd bought earlier. I was relatively sure nobody in here would have this dress. At least I'd be somewhat unique amongst the throngs of identikit teenagers that surrounded me.

Still, I decided to go and check out the huge display of accessories and make-up to see if there was anything I could spend my five pounds on. It was here that Mike finally caught up with me, as I studied an array of lip gloss colours. I was choosing between two near identical shades of pink when I felt that tell-tale hand on my shoulder. I still jumped a little, but it was a relief to find it was Mike and not another overly-familiar American.

'I came down because I didn't really think the stuff up there was meant for me.' said Mike.

'Yeah, same here to be honest. I think there's some seats over there.' I replied, still eager to browse the lip gloss in peace.

Mike did as instructed and walked over to a large upholstered cube that already had some other dads perched on it. They looked up and smiled at him briefly before returning their gaze to their respective smartphones.

I finalised my selection, opting for the lighter of the two pinks which I thought would complement my pale complexion and be more subtle than the darker, hotter pink I then discarded. I queued up at the counter and eventually paid using the crumpled five pound note. I strode out of the rope maze with a large bag with a solitary lip gloss in, plus all the leaflets and catalogues that accompany every purchase a girl makes. I made my way over to the upholstered cube.

'Ready?' asked Mike.

I nodded and we were once again on our way. Our last destination before heading back to the hotel was to be Oxford Street's flagship department store. One reason I'd bought the lip gloss was that I figured I'd struggle to find anything in the next store for less than a fiver, however much I wanted one of those little yellow bags to take my PE kit to school in next year.

Chapter 9

As we walked towards Bond Street the crowds were beginning to thin slightly and the heat, in turn, felt a little less oppressive. It was still warm and somewhat humid, but the direct sunlight had eased off and the odd breeze blew between buildings and whipped through my hair. I shifted my sunglasses up onto my head, to pin my hair into place and stop it fluttering in front of my eyes as we made our way across the roads laden with taxis, themselves in turn, laden with shopping bags. Of course Mike's cropped haircut and slim fitting polo shirts were designed for all weathers and made me jealous of the fact that men didn't need to gauge the wind-speed before leaving the house.

We arrived at the first set of glass doors, but Mike suggested we kept walking to the last set so we could look at the window displays. I was a little confused by his insistence on this, but as usual he was right. Mike had the inside knowledge that made our trip all the more interesting. I did wonder for a moment whether he'd been planning this trip with me for longer than he had let on. We stopped in front of the ornate window displays, all themed around summer and travel. Bespoke oversized designer shoes and handbags, giant beach towels and hampers, all helped to create a surreal diorama of the perfect summer holiday.

The displays had certainly whetted my appetite sufficiently and by the time we reached the last set of glass doors I was at the peak of my frenzy. It was all I could do to wait a few seconds for Mike before bursting through those doors. I needn't have been quite so excited since we were now in the homewares section, which although impressive and full of awesome looking kitchen gadgets, wasn't what I was hoping for when I entered.

We continued through the store towards a vast array of glass cabinets which I hoped contained jewellery, as I got nearer I began to see names I recognised, as well as a few I didn't, which worried me slightly. My fears proved well founded when I realised we were in the pens and stationery section. I was beginning to break out in a cold sweat, my pace quickened through this hall until I came to a set of escalators and a guide to the various floors. My eyes darted back and forth looking out for the key words from the list in my mind, handbags, shoes and designer dresses.

I span round to check I hadn't lost Mike but he was just behind me, looking a little out of breath as I'd just traipsed through the store like a woman possessed. He too studied the store guide before deciding to just follow me wherever I went. I opted for the handbags section first, planned my route and set off in the direction of my favourite designers.

What amazed me most about the displays I found when I arrived was just how sparsely populated they were. Sometimes a little three-walled concession store had approximately eight to ten handbags in it, which seemed like an awful waste of space to me. It also served to make each one seem like some fabled object, an important relic, or museum piece. Each bag was perched on its own tiny pedestal like the golden idol from Indiana Jones. I mulled over the possibility of replacing one with a bag of sand and making my getaway, but feared it may not be as easy as Indie made it look.

I could have spent hours in each little shop, stroking the supple lambs-leather and gasping at the price tags, but to be honest the security guards made me a little uncomfortable and seeing someone actually handing over their credit card to the shop assistant made it seem all too real. I couldn't quite rationalise spending a month's salary or two on a handbag, but somehow they had a allure to me that meant I too would gladly part with all my worldly possessions for the latest colour or style.

We moved on from handbags to the ladies shoe section, which was an enigma in itself. I soon noticed that there was a direct correlation between the height of the heel, the audacity of the design and the price. Simple flat ballet pumps were two or three hundred pounds, basic heels that might just be acceptable for school were four to five hundred, anything with five inch heels and spikes protruding from it seemed to ratchet the price up nearer four figures. I didn't think I could pull off the current 'meat tenderiser' trend. Maybe spiked shoes were supposed to be representative of female empowerment, but to be honest I enjoyed being looked after and doted on.

After staring at the shoes for a while, what I wanted to do next was go and try on a ridiculously expensive dress that I couldn't possibly afford to buy.

To do so might require some advance planning, so I considered how best to discuss this absurd request with Mike. I didn't want to appear ungrateful for the fabulous dress he'd bought me earlier that day. I also didn't want him to think I was materialistic. I did, however, really want to feel like a million dollars, if only for a millisecond.

'Mike...' I said, with a rising intonation that suggested I was about to ask a favour.

'Yes Princess?' he replied, in a tone of voice that suggested he wouldn't be able to say no.

'Can I go upstairs and try on a ridiculously expensive dress?' I blurted out, in a less considered manner than I'd rehearsed in my head.

Mike laughed a little and asked why that required his input. I explained that he'd have to come with me and at least give the impression that he might buy one, otherwise they might not let me try anything on.

I suggested he needed to remain calm and look casual, so at least one of us looked like we belonged up there amongst those sky-high designer prices. I felt sure I was going to be overwhelmed and frankly a bit giddy, I needed Mike as a sobering influence and I figured his indifference and disinterest could easily pass for nonchalance. He agreed and we set off ascending the escalators to the top floor, the number of shoppers reducing with every level we passed until we finally reached the summit.

No sooner had we disembarked the escalator on the top floor of the department store, than we were set upon by a tall sales assistant in an impeccably tailored pant suit. I froze but luckily my chaperone stepped up to the mark and batted away the assistant's question with aplomb.

'We're just browsing for now, we'll come and find you if we need any assistance.' he said almost rudely.

'Very good sir.' came the reply.

We walked briskly to the other side of the escalators as we didn't feel we could ask that member of staff for assistance now, even if we needed it. Luckily as we did so, we came across a few rails of dresses that were on sale and whose prices weren't completely beyond the reach of ordinary folk such as ourselves. Mike on the other hand didn't believe in doing things by halves and steered me away from the sale rail and into a separate little section through a grand stone archway, filled with the most glamorous evening wear I'd ever seen outside of magazines or television red-carpet coverage. Another assistant walked over towards us and again asked us if we needed any help.

'Yes please, my daughter has a birthday party to attend tonight at her friend's house and I'd like to buy her a new dress for the occasion,' said Mike unprompted, 'perhaps you could help us find something?'.

The bullishness of Mike's request ensured the assistant took it seriously and she asked a few additional questions to further identify my needs. Mike elaborated on this hypothetical party, it was to be from 6pm-9pm, predominantly indoors but also outside in the courtyard, dancing optional. The assistant then looked me up and down to gauge my size in an instant, before telling us to sit on a nearby sofa while she raced around to pick up half a dozen options. '*I could get used to this kind of service.*' I thought, although I wasn't sure they provided it in my local department store.

Mike and I staged a whispered conversation while the assistant was away, it purported to be about the party and what style of dress I wanted, but really it was more about my surprise at how he'd taken to his new role as wealthy father of a spoilt socialite daughter. He was indulging my fantasy in meticulous detail, except for where he kept calling me his daughter, of course. Still, I was enjoying being treated like a princess, even if I was yet to make him my prince.

'Ok,' said the assistant, 'I've got a few options for you here, let me know your initial thoughts and I can go and find some more based on your response to these.'

She beckoned me to stand up so she could first hold the dresses against me. I felt underdressed in my vest top and Capri pants but I suppose I couldn't very well be wearing an evening dress to go shopping for another evening dress.

'So the first one we have is a simple yet elegant dress in a dark charcoal colour, charcoal is very popular right now, it has all the slimming qualities of black but with a little more pop. I think this would look great as it pinches around the waist and would give you some hips.'

She highlighted this by running her fingers up and down the gap between my vest top and Capri pants in a strangely alluring way.

'Second is this midnight blue dress which finishes just above the knee, this is a bit more of a party dress, has a younger feel I think, I guess it depends on whether you want that or something a bit more classical though?'

'What do you think Dad?' I asked.

'I think the classical length, you have enough dresses like that navy one at home.' said Mike.

I smiled at him and stifled a giggle. He was even beginning to convince me with this act.

The assistant swapped some hangers around in her hands and called another assistant over to take the knee length dresses away. She now held the charcoal dress and one other, a scarlet-coloured dress with a split that ran from the calf to just above the knee. She held it against me and continued her sales spiel.

'Now this', she said confidently, 'I think would work really well for you. It can be quite hard to move about in a full length dress, especially if you're moving from indoors to outdoors and possibly dancing too. This would solve that problem and allow you a bit of movement, as well as accentuating your long slender legs. The neck line doesn't plunge down too far and would really make the most of your unblemished décolletage.

I was almost beginning to relinquish my feelings for Mike and fall for the saleswoman instead – she made me feel as good as anybody ever had about my frail, skinny body. For a moment I forgot she was trying to sell me a dress and instead hung on every word that came out of her mouth and cherished every hint of anything complimentary.

'Can I try this one on then?' I asked, pointing to the red one.

'Of course Miss, right this way,' said the assistant. 'I'll help her with the dress if that's ok, sir?'

Mike nodded and smiled as the woman led me away to a quieter corner of the store where the changing rooms were. I hadn't initially realised what the phrase 'help her with the dress' meant, or why she felt it necessary to ask Mike's permission. I was soon to find out though as the assistant pulled back a large velvet curtain, stepped in and turned to look at the sheepish girl still standing outside.

'In you come, Miss.' she said with a firm, yet pleasant tone of voice.

I followed her into the huge private changing room and she handed me the dress as she closed the curtain behind us. My heartbeat quickened, I hadn't ever got changed in front of anyone except my mum, and I hadn't done that for a while now. I sensed that the assistant's time was valuable and I didn't want to waste any. I had to pretend this was completely normal to me, otherwise she might suss that I was an impostor in this world of designer outfits and overtly complimentary shop assistants.

I started by removing my sandals, which I was able to kick off effortlessly much like I had on the grass outside Westminster. I then held the bottom of my vest top between my fingers, with my arms crossed, took a deep breath in and peeled it over my head. It wasn't as daunting as I thought it might be and the assistant was busying herself taking the dress off the hanger and carefully untying the tags, so they could be replaced as necessary. I breathed in again, this time only shallowly, to ease a thumb inside the waistband of my Capri pants. I used the leverage to undo the large button that fastened them at the front, before easing the zip downwards causing them to easily slip off my narrow hips.

I helped the Capri pants past my thighs and over my knees and stepped out of them, before kicking them aside. The assistant stepped over and picked them up from the floor and folded them while I stood motionless in my underwear. It was right at this very moment that I thanked my lucky stars that I'd ditched all my plain white cotton underwear from my bag at my father's house, as I felt sure I'd have opted to wear them today in this sweltering heat. As it was, I stood now in a matching bra and knicker set of lilac with a white pinstripe, looking rather pleased with my choice.

'You'd probably be best taking your underwear off to get a true representation of what the dress will look like, it's quite close-fitting and you won't want straps and lines showing.' said the assistant, still folding my clothes and partially averting her gaze.

'You'd generally wear a dress like this without underwear, certainly without a bra, maybe with a very sheer pair of knickers if you prefer. You don't have to though, if you'd prefer to try it on as you are for now?'

Relieved, I nodded at the latter suggestion and informed her that was exactly what I'd like to do. It was either that or run out of the changing rooms without looking back.

The assistant gathered up the dress and squatted down on the floor in front of me, urging me to step into the ruffled pile of scarlet material. I did so and before I knew it she'd raised the dress up around me, brought herself behind and offered me a hole to put my arm through. I did as instructed, first one, then the other, as the dress was hooked onto my shoulders. She gathered up my hair and pulled it tight to one side and offered it to me to hold. I was glad to take it out of her hands as she had yanked it pretty hard.

As I relaxed my grip and held it off to one side she pushed the fingers of one hand against the small of my back and zipped up the dress in one smooth motion. She was right, I did need help with the dress. She grabbed my hair back from me and fanned it over my back and shoulders before forcibly spinning me round to observe myself in the mirror as she stepped aside.

The room fell silent, I stared at the beautiful woman looking back at me, a visage of near perfection. As I admired myself in the dress the assistant admired her own handiwork from behind. She looked almost as happy as I did as I caught her eye in the mirror.

'It's beautiful isn't it?' she asked.

'Yes,' I replied, 'and so am I...' I continued under my breath.

Just as I was beginning to think I couldn't possibly look any better, I noticed the strap of my bra poking out from one side of the dress. Then I turned 90 degrees to the side and looked back over my shoulder at my bum. I could indeed see the tell-tale line of the hem of my knickers protruding through the side of the clingy dress. The assistant looked at me once again as if to say 'I told you so', before offering me another chance at redemption.

'Shall we try it without the underwear?' she asked again, more insistent this time.

'Yes.' I replied, more confidently than I imagined I would.

The assistant raced up behind me and unzipped the dress halfway down my back and began unclasping my bra before I could even think of doing so myself. She did so with one hand and far more efficiently than I could have. Her fingers were soft against my skin and I felt a strange tingle at having my bra unclasped for the first time by another person.

She peeled the dress off my shoulders and motioned to me to put one arm first out of the dress and then out of my bra. She hooked the dress back onto that shoulder and then did the same on the other side. She then unzipped the dress a little further and began hitching up the bottom of it to just above my knees and commanding me to reach up from the front to remove my knickers. I did so extremely inefficiently but I was glad she'd allowed me to do at least that part myself. I stepped out of them and stood to one side. The assistant immediately let go of the gathered dress which fell to the floor, then zipped it to the top once again, before picking up my knickers and folding them. It was probably the first time they'd ever been folded.

As she stepped away again I looked back at myself in the mirror. I didn't really look any different, except for the lack of straps and lines, although the act of the sales assistant undoing my bra had caused my nipples to become slightly stiffer. They now protruded through the delicate fabric that created a minute barrier between them and the open air.

'You can get some tape for those.' said the assistant, motioning with her eyes towards my chest. 'It will stop them from looking quite as prominent'. I didn't know whether I was more perturbed by her looking at my nipples, or that there was a product specifically designed for the purpose of covering them up.

'Do you want me to get your Dad to have a look?' came the assistant's next question.

'No, it's ok.' I replied, mortified at the thought.

I then realised that if I was ever going to get Mike to look at me objectively – to consider me a potential partner instead of a dependent – it would be now.

'Actually, yes, ok, I guess he should see it first.' I followed with quickly.

'Of course, you wait here and I'll go and get him.' she said, disappearing through the edge of the curtain.

Chapter 10

I hadn't really thought through the ramifications of the question the assistant had asked me. I now had to stand completely still – for what would likely be a minute or two – dreading what was about to happen. Mike was about to walk in, to see me in a beautiful long red dress, with a split up one side to just above the knee, my nipples clearly visible through the thin veil of material and a pile of my underwear on a chair over to one side.

I began to breathe more deeply and with increasing regularity. Before long I was practically hyperventilating. It was too late to change my mind now. At any moment the man I had come to see as my potential suitor was about to walk through that curtain. He was Mike the guardian, Mike the friend, Mike my dad in this elaborate ruse, but also 'Shower Mike', the object of my affection. He was all of those people and all of them were about to see me at once, at my best and my worst, at my most confident *and* my most vulnerable.

Before I had a chance to consider it any further there he was, staring at me once again. His eyes this time didn't start at the floor and work their way up, they started at my nervous eyes, then my nervous smile, then back to my nervous eyes again. They then made a short trip around to survey my figure in the dress, before returning briskly to my eyes. He too seemed uncomfortable as he spoke.

'Very nice, Princess.' he said, before making brief eye contact with the assistant and high-tailing it out of the changing room.

I had to say, I was a little disappointed by his reaction. As the assistant closed the curtain again she turned back to look at me and offered some words of comfort.

'Sometimes it's difficult for dad's to see their daughters looking so grown up.' she said. 'I'm sure he thought you looked pretty, but it's not always easy for dads to say things like that.'

'Thanks.' I replied, all too aware that in this instance, that clearly wasn't the problem.

The assistant asked if I was ready to take the dress off, I nodded solemnly. She unzipped the back all the way down and grazed my bottom with her hand as she did so. I barely noticed. I let her take the dress off my shoulders and allowed it to fall all the way to just above the floor where the assistant's hands were waiting to catch it. This time I stepped out of the dress and stood naked in front of her, she folded the dress over her arm and handed me my underwear which I put on haphazardly before reaching for the rest of my clothes. I left the assistant in the changing room putting the dress back on its hanger and affixing the tags once again. I walked out to look for Mike, who was no longer on the sofa where he had previously sat.

I didn't feel like stopping and trying to catch sight of him, so instead I walked in a zig-zag fashion around the various boutiques towards the escalators hoping instead that he'd spot me. I arrived at the huge store guide sign and stood waiting for Mike. He arrived a few seconds later to find a glum looking girl with one foot up, leaning against the sign.

'I'm sorry about that Becky,' he said, 'I didn't mean to walk out like that. I just didn't know where to look if I'm honest.'

'I'm sorry too,' I replied. 'The assistant asked if she should go and get you and I thought, if we were pretending that you were going to buy it, I should say yes. I didn't think it would be that awkward for you. I guess I just hoped to be told that I looked nice or something.'

'I know,' said Mike, 'I just didn't know whether I should be the person to say something like that.'

'Well who else is going to say it?' I snapped.

I was upset now and could feel my eyes getting teary and averted my gaze down to the floor.

'You're right.' said Mike, dejectedly.

I uncrossed my arms in order to wipe my eyes, as I did so Mike grabbed the fingers of my left hand with his. He waited for me to finish wiping away the solitary tear that had formed before delicately holding my right hand too between his fingers. I found myself looking up at him as he did this.

'You looked beautiful Rebecca.'

He leaned in towards me and moved his head in a dramatic arc to one side, before planting a soft kiss on my left cheek as he continued to hold my hands. He arced away again, smiled at me and grasped my fingers with his before asking if I was ok. I wriggled my hands out of his, violently, causing him to recoil slightly as if I were about to hit him and storm off.

I wasn't about to do that though. He had, in that moment, reaffirmed everything I thought about him and everything I had dreamed about. I flung my arms around him and buried my head in his chest for the second time in a few days. This time he didn't move or hold my head against himself, he just let me get a good squeeze in before I relinquished my grip and smiled at him. Before he could say a word I had jumped on the escalator down to the next floor and left him behind.

I waited until I'd got to the bottom of the escalator and composed myself before I finally turned round to see Mike about halfway down.

'Let's head back to the hotel.' I said with a spring in my step.

'You've perked up a bit.' Mike responded, 'I'm glad you're ok now.'

'I am. Thanks.'

I linked arms with him again and we headed around the helter-skelter of escalators to the bottom floor.

Upon our arrival back out on the street we were hit by a wave of humidity and then – worse still – spots of rain. Rain on a hot summer's day feels like a distinctly British thing, we don't have a monsoon season, we just have all the various weather types all year round, sometimes with no discernible seasons at all. Warm rain is just about the worst kind though, catching you by surprise as it so often does.

The rain wasn't heavy, but that didn't stop the vast majority of pedestrians cramming themselves under the nearest available shop awning or into doorways, nearly carrying us back into the department store we'd just left. We had to fight to get out into the rain, which seemed counter-intuitive, but necessary nonetheless. Luckily we could walk the shorter distance to Bond Street station and get the tube from there instead of trekking back to Oxford Circus. We hurried along the outside of the pavement, risking getting splashed by taxis that crawled along the kerb through the freshly-formed puddles.

Upon reaching the station we had to queue to get in, as countless other shoppers had decided that enough was enough and the mass migration of people back to their hotels and houses began. We finally got under cover just as the rain was coming down a little heavier. I nearly slipped walking down the final few treacherous steps towards the ticket barriers. Mike handed me my travel card, which he had kept secure each time we left the underground, and we relaxed a bit and allowed ourselves to saunter towards the platform.

Waiting for our next train I raised the topic of finding a supermarket near the hotel once again.

'Oh yeah,' said Mike, 'I think there's one near the tube station we get off at, only a small one mind you.'

'Cool,' I replied, 'I'm sure it'll be big enough for what we want.'

I didn't particularly want anything from this shop after all, I was just keen to make sure Mike found some beers he liked as he'd missed out earlier. I was tempted though, to see whether he'd buy something for me too. Drinking alcohol seemed an integral part of being a grown-up. I felt compelled to try to join in this ritual in order to ease my passage into adulthood, and by doing so, further cement my burgeoning romantic relationship with Mike.

The tube train pulled into the station and it took the noise and sudden flash of colour before my eyes to snap me out of another daydream. We prised ourselves onto a packed carriage which forced us to stand extremely close together, not that I was going to complain about that. In fact I deliberately stood with my back to Mike and made sure when the train pulled away sharply that I fell back against him briefly. It was these little moments of contact that titillated me and, I hoped, stirred a little something in him at least.

We clambered off the last of our tube trains for the day and I wasn't disappointed to have left that part of the journey behind. We climbed an assortment of escalators and made our way up to street-level to look for the nearest supermarket. The rain had eased off, with only the odd spot coming down, although each drop was larger and seemed to contain as much rain as multiple smaller drops. One went down the front of my vest and I squealed audibly, thrusting a hand in after it to try and mop it up. Mike stood a few feet away, on the street corner, convinced he knew where he was going. It was times like this I wish I'd remembered to bring my smartphone instead of that ancient thing Mike had given me.

We walked down a nearby street, right to the bottom, where it intersected with a main road. Further along we spied our supermarket and hurried in to get away from the last vestiges of rain. Mike headed straight for the alcohol aisle, I for the snacks and crisps section. I found some tortilla chips which came free when you bought the dip, it seemed like an irresistible offer to me. I picked them up and headed back over to Mike who was still studying the various bottled beers. They seemed to have a good selection as the supermarket was running some kind of beer festival promotion for the summer – Mike was enjoying reading the off-beat names.

After selecting two bottles, Rusty Beaver and Wizard's Sleeve, Mike turned to me and asked if I wanted anything. I was to be hopelessly out of depth in my response to that question. Like every teenager who walks into a pub having watched too many soaps and simply says "pint please", I coughed and spluttered something about alcoholic lemonade.

'Ok,' said Mike, 'I'm unsure where that will be.'

He glanced around at the shelves before finding a large bottle of lemonade, on which the label designers had drawn sunglasses onto lemons, to signify that they were cool and thus alcoholic. He picked up the two litre bottle and showed it to me. I nodded to signify that was the correct thing and he put it into the basket alongside his beers.

We made our way over to the checkouts and used the self-serve machines which bleeped noisily as soon as we started scanning the alcohol. A spotty lad sauntered over to us and waved his keys in front of the screen without so much as making eye contact with us. He seemed more focused on stopping the bleeping than verifying our ages. Mike put it all on his credit card as usual and we headed out of the shop in the direction of our hotel.

I felt sure tonight's dinner, although far less glamourous, would in some ways be a lot more grown-up. Without waiters there to embarrass me I could relax a bit more, really talk to my companion. Plus with the additional of alcohol – the social lubricant – there was no reason I couldn't enact step two of my plan.

Chapter 11

It had started spitting again for the last few steps of our journey back to the hotel so we scurried into the foyer and made our way up the staircase in the corner. We delved into our pockets simultaneously and pulled out our key cards, swiped them in perfect unison and headed into our rooms. I went straight for the adjoining door and unlocked my side, Mike did the same and swung it ajar before propping it open with a doorstop he'd found in the cupboard.

'Shower first?' said Mike with little droplets of rain still cascading down his forehead.

'*Are you offering?*' I thought, before replying with a more conventional 'Yes'.

We both walked away from the adjoining door and in the direction of our respective bathrooms, with the plan to reconvene ten or fifteen minutes later to start planning dinner. After a long day and plenty of walking I couldn't bear to stand in the shower for longer than was absolutely necessary, so I stripped off, jumped in, made light work of washing and jumped back out again after a few short minutes. I wrapped a towel around my damp hair and one around my body. I hadn't thought to bring any spare clothes with me into the bathroom so I tucked one corner of the towel in firmly at the side before walking towards the door.

It then occurred to me that I hadn't closed the adjoining door between our rooms. I listened for the sound of Mike's shower running, but I couldn't hear anything. I pressed my ear against the inside of the bathroom door, still nothing. I doubted he was in my room but I couldn't be too careful. I called out gently through the bathroom door and waited for a response. None came, so I bravely headed out to pick up some clothes from my suitcase.

As I stepped out into the hallway towards the bedroom area I could hear footsteps, and no sooner had I reached the adjoining doorway than Mike had burst through and bumped straight into me.

'Oops, sorry Becky, I thought I heard you calling me?' said Mike before turning around quickly and walking back into his room, closing the adjoining door behind him this time.

'I was calling out to make sure you *weren't* in my room so I could come out and get my clothes.' I shouted back through the door.

Mike laughed before adding 'At least we're even now!'

I guess that was indeed one way of looking at it, we'd each bumped into one another with nothing but a towel wrapped around us, but I still felt I had got the better end of the bargain. Despite the adjoining door now being closed I'd had enough of changing in public today so I headed back into the bathroom with some clean underwear, a pair of leggings and a loose fitting t-shirt, to get dressed. When I returned to the bedroom I knocked on the adjoining door to make sure it was safe to open. I headed into Mike's room and sat on the end of the bed.

'So, shall we have a look through the room service menu?' I asked.

'Yeah, here you take this one, I'll grab the one from your room.' replied Mike.

I sat and perused the 'Traditional' section of the menu as we'd discussed. Mike returned, sat on the bed and leant against the pillows behind me, his legs stretched out across the length of the bed. I turned round from my position to face him and crossed my legs as I sat with the menu on my lap.

'I quite fancy the fish and chips.' said Mike cheerily. 'How about you? What do you fancy?'

I looked up from my menu towards him, I couldn't give the obvious answer that my brain seemed intent on forcing me to vocalise. Instead, I looked back down at the menu without answering and mumbled something incoherent to signal that I was still undecided. Eventually I piped up, not to place my order, but rather to question Mike's.

'We can get good fish and chips back home.' I said.

'Yeah, that's true, but the heart wants what the heart wants! Maybe I'm homesick!' said Mike.

I chuckled to myself and carried on studying the menu, thinking more about the 'heart wants what the heart wants' mantra than about what to have for dinner. Then my stomach started to rumble loudly, causing me to shift my sitting position to try and mask the sound before making a snap decision of what to order.

'I'll have the steak and kidney pie please.' I said.

'Ok, we'll have it at the table over there by the window. Do you want to go and clear all the leaflets and stuff off it for me, while I ring down to reception?'

I cleared the table as instructed, brought an additional chair from my room into Mike's and rearranged the table and chairs so that we could both fit around them. I made sure we were sat opposite each other, with the window to our side. I stepped back and looked quite pleased with myself for creating this intimate and romantic dining space. From where I stood I noticed Mike's bed in my peripheral vision. '*One step at a time.*' I thought. I hoped that the sight of the bed wouldn't distract me during dinner and that his company would be stimulating enough.

I could hear Mike relaying the order to the woman on reception, he was using his best phone voice to do so. He said please and thank you more times in a minute than I had in my entire life. Not that I'm impolite, just that I tend to nod and smile as a default expression of gratitude. He finished up the phone call by repeating back the timeframe the receptionist had given him.

'Forty-five minutes, yes that's great, thank you. Goodbye.'

He replaced the handset and turned round to see me standing by the rearranged table and chairs, I did so with the customary wide-armed presentation gesture and a silent 'ta-da' etched on my face.

'Haha that's great Becky, thanks for doing that.' said Mike, smiling.

Forty-five minutes seemed like a long time to sit and wait for our dinner to arrive, so I suggested we flick the television on for a bit to pass the time. The first programme that came on was local news, which I sensed Mike would want to watch, so I left it on that channel, swivelled the TV towards the window and sat back in my chair at the dining table. Mike wandered around the room, picking up clothes, tidying papers away, making sure his room was clean before the room service came. The news was pretty insignificant, it had clearly been a slow day, although Mike suggested that it was often like this at weekends when the newsrooms run with a skeleton staff.

I stared blankly at the television for a while, as if trying to mentally tune it into something more interesting, then I perked up when I heard the clink of bottles. Mike had found the carrier bag with the drinks and was setting them onto the table before heading to the bathroom. He returned with the glass that hotels usually provide you to put your toothbrush in and set it on the table.

'I'll just go and get the one from your room.' he said, before heading through the adjoining door.

I was daydreaming at the time so it took me a few seconds to process what he'd said. I didn't have time to stop him but he was about to venture into my bathroom which, as well as generally being a complete mess, also still had my lilac underwear that I'd worn that day on the floor. A horrified and embarrassed look came across my face as he returned with the second glass.

I got up from the table without saying anything and headed back into my room. I made straight for the bathroom to see where I'd left my underwear and hoped they were somewhat concealed under a towel. I couldn't find them anywhere for some reason, but I didn't remember picking them up either. I walked back out into the bedroom and spotted them folded up on top of my bag. It was the second time today someone had picked up my worn underwear from the floor, it wasn't any less embarrassing than the first. I walked over and stuffed them into my bag so I wouldn't have another reminder of the incident.

I made my way back into Mike's room and sat down again at the table. He had poured me a large glass of alcoholic lemonade and half of one of the bottles of beer into his glass. I sipped at my drink, it was certainly fizzy and fruity enough, but had a bit more of a kick than the ones I was used to. I reached for the bottle and spun it round to read the back but it didn't make much sense to me, I wasn't sure what the strength of the one my Mum used to buy was. It tasted nice regardless, so I took a bigger gulp this time and sat back to continue watching the news.

Mike was sat on the bed a few feet away from me with his camera in hand, studying the pictures he'd taken that morning on its LCD screen. Without warning he pressed a button to switch it back to camera mode, turned it in my direction and shouted 'Smile!'. I instinctively turned and smiled, offering up my glass as if to say 'cheers' as he pressed the shutter to capture that moment. I felt a sense of pride that he'd want to take a picture of me at all, let alone one so mundane.

Minutes later there was a knock on the door, followed by a voice proclaiming it to be room service. Mike shuffled over to the door and opened it. A man wheeled into the room a little cart with two large plates with cloches atop. He continued to wheel it past the bed and over to the table before setting down the two plates and reversing his way out of the room. Mike locked the door behind him and walked back over to join me at the table for dinner.

'Well this was a really good idea Becky, thanks again for coming up with it.' said Mike, revealing his fish and chips from under its plastic cover.

'That's ok,' I replied, 'you've been really supportive these last few days and I just wanted to do something nice for you. I don't have the money to pay for it, but it's the thought that counts right?!'

'Absolutely. You can be such a sweet girl sometimes, I'm really sorry things aren't working out for you at your father's.'

'Yeah, me too. I guess we kinda got off on the wrong foot. I'll never really be able to forgive him for leaving Mum and me. But enough about him, I came here to get away from all that, let's talk about us.'

'Us?' replied Mike, slightly unsure of where the conversation was going.

'Yeah, us.' I said 'I hope we'll always be close'.

Maybe it was the lemonade talking, but I suddenly felt – as I stared at Mike from across the table – that the conversation should be about more than just this trip. Our future surely had to extend past this weekend.

'You'll always be a significant part of my life Becky,' came his response, 'probably more than you'll ever know.'

'What do you mean?' I asked.

'Oh, nothing really. Anyway, in a few years' time you'll be older and heading off to University or whatever. You might not want me in your life by then, cramping your style!'

'Awww don't say that. I put up with you cramping my style now don't I?' I said, winking at him as I sipped my drink.

'Haha, that's true I guess. I'll always be here for you Becky, you know that.'

I smiled and raised my glass of lemonade to toast that sentiment.

'To us...' said Mike as he clinked his glass into mine.

'...and growing older.' I added.

When he talked about always being there for me, I really hoped it was true. I couldn't imagine my life without him, in whatever capacity, but as I spent time close to him these last few days, I was beginning to struggle to think of any life other than the one I had written in my mind. I replayed our short conversation in my head as we tucked into our dinner. *I'll always be a significant part of his life... more than I'll ever know'*. That was a strange thing to say, I would have to press him further on it to find out exactly what he meant. For now though, I was content with his words and also with my rather delicious steak and kidney pie.

After a physically strenuous day walking around London, we didn't stop to talk much more during dinner, except to ask how each other's food was. We munched our way through the rather large portions pretty quickly and I was more than satisfied at the end of it. Mike cleared the plates onto a tray, took them outside and put them in the hallway, so that the room wouldn't smell too bad. It was a little late for that, so we closed the adjoining door to at least stop the competing scents of vinegar and gravy from wafting into my room, then opened the window the maximum two inches allowed by most modern hotels.

The air was still and no breeze entered through the tiny gap in the window, but it did allow the smell to escape somewhat, as well as increasing the level of street noise significantly. It was nice to hear the faint sound of car horns and engines, the occasional siren from an emergency service vehicle, it reminded you that you were in a big city, an epicentre of culture and business. Once again I felt a part of something larger, a greater plan, a feeling I rarely had when sitting around in the small back-bedroom at home.

I turned my chair slightly closer to Mike's in order to get a better view out of the window, urging him to do the same. We now sat at about a forty-five degree angle to each other, identifying buildings in the background and trying to guess where we'd walked today and what sort of distance we'd covered. It was the kind of idle chit-chat reserved for after dinner, when the fullness of the stomach dictates the slowness of the synapses in the brain. I doubted I'd remember the details of this conversation in the same way as I did the one just prior.

Mike topped up our glasses for the last time. After dinner he'd moved onto the second of his oddly named beers and was finishing up the last few dregs of the bottle. He poured me another large glass of lemonade and noticed that around three quarters of the bottle had gone. I too had noticed how much of it I'd drunk, but was deliberately not drawing attention to it. He drunk the last of the beer and poured the remainder of the lemonade for himself – I suspected – as a form of damage control.

It was too late though, I'd drunk more alcohol than I had for a long time, possibly more than I had ever drunk before in one evening. I felt a little light headed, but pleasantly so, with a warm aura radiating from inside my chest. The delicate balance of the cool air from the open window, combined with the warmth from the alcohol, seemed to keep the rest of my body at the perfect ambient temperature. A calmness descended over me, one that belied words, causing me to stare out of the window and pray that the moment never passed.

Out of the corner of one eye I could see Mike looking at his watch. I didn't want to know what time it was, I felt sure that whatever his next words, they would inevitably lead to the end of our evening.

Instead he looked away from his watch and across to me, then back out of the window, saying nothing. I breathed in deeply through my nose and closed my eyes momentarily, as I did so I felt the room was spinning slightly off axis and so quickly reopened them.

By now, after a litre and a half of alcoholic lemonade, my bladder was as full as my stomach. The sense that I'd need the toilet was beginning to occupy my otherwise wonderfully vacant mind. Once I'd thought about it I couldn't ignore it. I was going to have to get up in a minute and when I did so I felt sure I was going to struggle to walk in a straight line, even the short distance to the bathroom. I didn't want Mike to know I was a little tipsy, especially on alcoholic lemonade. I stayed motionless in my chair hoping he'd get up first.

The war of bladder attrition probably lasted only a few minutes, but it felt much longer. Eventually he did get up and walked in the direction of his bathroom. I waited until he was safely out of view before leaping up myself which, with hindsight, was a mistake.

I had to stay stationary in an upright position for a few seconds before I felt confident enough to walk again. I managed to walk in a surprisingly straight line but it felt like I was zig-zagging across the hallway to the bathroom. I was glad of the rest when I sat down to go to the toilet, neglecting to close the bathroom door. Luckily, the sound – which was louder than usual – was drowned out by the flushing of Mike's toilet next door.

I got back to my feet and decided that I should probably have a lie down, regardless of what time it was now. So I walked back to the adjoining doorway and propped myself up against it to say goodnight to Mike. He informed me that we didn't need to get up early in the morning, which was like music to my warm clothy ears. I closed the door and locked it, before spinning round on my heels and lying face down on top of my bed. My mind wanted to sleep but I would soon find that my body had other ideas.

Chapter 12

As soon as I'd laid face down on the bed, I realised I wasn't in the most comfortable position and turned over onto my back and laid out flat, my head just below the pillow. The warmth from the alcohol that seemed to radiate from my vital organs, was now causing even my extremities to overheat. I no longer had the balancing cool air from the open window and I couldn't muster up the energy to go and open mine. Instead I lay there for a moment, cursing my own laziness, before deciding to get undressed in order to solve the problem.

I wanted to remain as still as possible and so I started by bending each leg up alongside me in turn, digging my thumb into each sock at the heel and prizing them off one at a time. My toes wiggled, almost involuntarily, in glee at their new found freedom. I now felt about five percent cooler but still fifty percent too hot. I raised up on my heels and pinned my shoulders into the mattress, forcing my stomach and bottom up into the air. This time I scraped both thumbnails down to prise my leggings and knickers away from the small of my back and pushed them halfway down my legs. I left them there for the time being, covering my lower legs and binding them together at the knees.

I felt marginally cooler now but this hadn't helped the burning sensation in my torso, so I quickly grabbed at my t-shirt and began to take it off, shifting my body up off the mattress by minuscule amounts each time I needed to move it further up. Once it had reached my shoulders I was able to arch my neck forward slightly to raise them off the bed and get the t-shirt over my head. As it came off, my head and neck snapped back onto the bed and I transferred the t-shirt from one arm to the other before throwing it onto the floor by the window.

Still not satisfied, and feeling I could be cooler, I leaned my left shoulder across my right, so my upper body was on its side, before reaching around to unclasp my bra with one hand. It wasn't as easy as the sales assistant had made it look and I soon had to sit bolt upright and use two hands to undo it. I threw it onto the pile of clothes that was building up on the floor and laid back down on the bed. I felt much cooler now, there's a certain liberating feeling when you're not wearing a bra, nothing to do with feminism, just the physiological reaction to fresh air running beneath and between your breasts.

I lay like this for a few more seconds, before realising that I wanted to free the remaining parts of my body, which were currently linked together by the elasticated Lycra between my knees. I attempted to bring my left knee up as high as I could, out of the leggings slightly, which allowed me to push it down over the calf to the ankle. From there I arched both legs to the side of me and slipped both the leggings and my knickers over one ankle and off the foot completely. I then straightened my body out and used my newly freed left foot, instead of my hand, to push the right side of my leggings and knickers down the leg, over the calf and off the foot. I left a few short centimetres on my toes, which I hoped would provide enough friction to swing the remainder over to the pile by the window.

I swung my right leg violently across the bed and, sure enough, extricated myself from the last item of clothing, which rather neatly landed atop the existing pile of clothes. I now lay completely free from cotton and Lycra, polyester and elastic, spread-eagled across the entire surface of the large king-sized bed. I could feel the heat escaping from the previously covered patches of skin, replaced by fresh, cool air which made the tiny, almost imperceptible hairs that covered my body stand on end. I felt satisfied that I had done all I could to cool myself down, but there was one last part of me that still felt warmer than usual – one I couldn't as easily attribute to the alcohol in my blood.

I reached down with my right hand, stretched out my palm and held it flat, a centimetre or so away from my body. The change in temperature wasn't perceptible, but I felt it ought to be given the fierce heat I now felt between my legs. It wasn't a constant heat, more a pulsating one, like an oscillating red light, appearing to glow each time it span through one complete revolution and met the eye. I allowed the palm of my hand to approach my skin more closely, subtly monitoring the change in temperature as I did so, until finally it came to rest against the warm pink flesh.

The warmth I felt dissipated slightly, some of it transferring to my palm, some seeming to make its way up my stomach and chest, forcing a sharp intake of breath which I held for a moment. The same wave of energy rattled my brain and momentarily forced my eyelids to clasp tightly shut. Seconds later I was able to breathe out, open my eyes and take stock of the situation. I knew what was happening to me, but I wasn't sure what to do about it. I'd felt this warmth before, but usually only for a fleeting moment, never for a prolonged period like this. The intense heat felt like a beacon, guiding me towards it, the brief release of energy I'd had when placing my hand upon the source, told me that I was in the right place and beckoned me to explore the surface further.

My palm was still pressed against the pink flesh, but having held it in one place for a minute or so, the sensation had passed. When I moved my hand away a sudden rush of cold air seemed to graze the surface and fire up the beacon once again. This time I pressed the heel of my palm against the flesh a little more forcibly and ran it slowly down the length of the soft skin, causing it to buckle and swell at the sides as I did so. Every millimetre I touched sent a bold new signal through my nervous system and to my brain, as if it were being touched for the first time. Of course none of these parts were being touched for the first time, but for some reason, with this heat and my state of mind, I couldn't convince my brain otherwise.

The fact that each millimetre of my skin felt brand new caused me to ponder using the tips of my fingers to heighten the sensation and explore myself in more detail. I stretched out my index finger and tucked in the remaining fingers except for the thumb which I rested against my lower stomach. I hovered the extended finger over the area briefly while I contemplated my actions. I took a deep breath and pushed my finger against the slight gap where the two halves met – causing them to separate slightly more – then dragged the finger up from the bottom to the top, along this newly formed ridge. The natural arc of the movement of my finger eased a passage away, before it had reached the join at the top.

This brief journey for my index finger had indeed given new and more minutely detailed sensory signals to my brain. The touch of my finger, despite my having extremely soft hands, still felt slightly rough against this most sensitive area of skin. So, before its second tour of duty, I felt compelled to put the tip of my finger into my mouth in order to wet it slightly and reduce the friction against my delicate skin. I made exactly the same arc as before, but this time as my finger reached forty-five degrees the lack of resistance caused it to push slightly deeper into the crevice between the two halves of flesh. As it did so it met with an even warmer area, this time with its own natural lubricant which covered the tip of my finger, including the nail.

As my finger had finished its second exploratory journey, I suddenly became aware of the limpness of my left hand, which, throughout this process, had lay motionless on the bed, next to my body. My focussing on it caused it to spring into life and find a new home, bent at the elbow and with the hand flat against my right breast, the nipple burrowed dead centre in my palm and the fingers tucked fractionally under my armpit. From this position it monitored my increasing heart rate. The data, however, would soon become lost inside my scrambled brain.

I readied myself for another, more studied and possibly deeper exploration of my body, popping my index finger back into my mouth to prepare it as before. This time it tasted different, salty yet faintly sweet, with an unusual texture. The sensation on my tongue was simultaneously pleasant yet unpleasant, like eating a piece of salted caramel. I gave it no further thought, as I relished the prospect of touching myself again.

This time the beckoning heat guided my finger straight for the area at the top where the two halves meet, an area which, if possible, was even hotter, seeming like the burning centre of the beacon, or the bulb of the oscillating red light. As my finger merely rested against it, the sensation was almost unbearable, here, unlike the rest of the area between my legs, I seemed to be able to distinguish fractions of millimetres. It was as if each time I breathed, my finger, although seeming to remain still, moved a minuscule amount, the perception of which was only made possible by the wave of energy coursing through my entire body.

My left hand pressed closer against my breast, squashing it slightly against my chest, as the index finger on my right hand began to become more brave with its movements. First I ran the rounded surface of the finger left to right over this red bulb, before making the journey back slightly more quickly from right to left. I could feel my heart rate increasing and my breathing become more and more shallow and frequent. The sounds of both my breathing and heartbeat were becoming deafening – a cacophonous noise surrounding my ear drums, permeating from the inside, stopping any noise from elsewhere in the room, or the street outside, from getting in, like when your head slips under the water level in the bath.

My index finger now began making circular movements, as if trapped in a vortex or whirlpool, the epicentre of which, the red bulb, was relentlessly guiding it in, like the sirens on the rocks. I was powerless to stop, despite the warnings being given off by my heart and lungs, the vociferousness of which was dwarfed by the pleasure receptors in my brain demanding I continue. By now the sensation was eighty percent pleasure and twenty percent pain, having shifted from ninety and ten only moments ago. Despite the increase in discomfort, the ability I had to ignore it had increased in equal measure. I found myself occasionally holding my breath for eight to ten seconds at a time, in order to quell the negative feelings and allow me to carry on, though this only served to further quicken my heart rate.

I had never felt so in tune with my body, to the detriment of awareness of my surroundings. My eyes had remained open for most of this time, but my vision had blurred at the edges, only a narrow band of definition existed down the centre of my chest and between my thighs. As long as my brain could process this light into a barely three dimensional image, the rest was simply distraction.

Wave after wave of energy pulsed over my body, the distance between the waves shortened and the peaks and troughs steepened. The energy reached the tips of my toes and beckoned me to stretch them out to maximise the time before each wave left them. It reached my shoulders and neck and created spasms which pinned my shoulder blades into the bed behind me and shifted the crown of my head down into the pillow, extending my chin up away from my chest and resulting in my eyes now looking away from my body and at the wall behind. My eyes picked a new point of focus, a singular point on the white-washed wall. I held my breath again and the point became smaller and smaller, until, like everything else, it turned black. All around was blackness.

When I came to, I checked the clock by my bedside, it was now 11:30pm. I was sure I hadn't come to bed that late. My mouth was dry, my head was pounding and my entire body was flushed red and covered in goose-bumps. I cast my mind back to the last thing I remembered before the blackness, to what I'd been doing moments before. I sat up, still groggy and a little dazed, reached for a bottle of water that was warm from sitting out so long and took a sip. If that was what it felt like to have an orgasm it wasn't something I was keen to repeat any time soon.

Chapter 13

I woke up early – early for a Sunday morning anyway – at around 8am, but I wasn't in any hurry to get up and get dressed. I reached for the television remote control from the bedside table and pressed the on/off button. At first nothing seemed to be happening, the red light at the bottom came on but the screen remained black. I lay my head back down on the pillow in defeat. No sooner had I done so than I was being startled into life by the morning news presenter, who was now staring straight at me and bellowing the morning's headlines directly into my ear canals. I frantically grabbed the remote and after a few seconds of unsuccessfully looking for the volume button, I instead opted to hit the on/off button again. The ensuing silence was glorious, but it didn't last as long as I'd hoped.

'Becky?' came a voice through the adjoining door.

'Morning!' I replied. 'Sorry, I couldn't find the button to turn it down.'

'That's ok, the TV did the same to me yesterday the first time I put it on.' said Mike. 'I'm gonna head down for a swim and a sauna in a bit, do you wanna come with me?'

I considered his proposal, it was a little early for me, but my heart was beating so fast since the TV had come on so loudly that I figured I might as well utilise the energy. I was still feeling grotty from the previous night, a combination of the alcohol and what had happened afterwards. Maybe a swim and a sauna would be cleansing, both physically and spiritually.

'Becky?' came the voice through the door again.

'Yeah ok, I'll be about 15 minutes if that's alright?' I replied.

'Sure, just come into my room when you're ready, I'll unlock the door.' said Mike.

I threw back the covers unabashed, then ashamedly clutched them over myself again, before much less dramatically shifting to the edge of the bed and reaching for my suitcase to look for my new bikini. I put the bottoms on first before standing up and trying desperately to tie up the back of the bikini top. I hadn't done a very good job but it was at least tight enough not to fall off now. Over the top I put on the t-shirt and leggings from the pile by the window and walked into the bathroom to make sure I wasn't too dishevelled. Unfortunately I was, but fortunately I was also too tired to care. I simply brushed my hair with my fingers, tucked it behind my ears, and headed back into the bedroom to find my sandals.

I unlocked my side of the adjoining door and stepped through to find Mike sitting silently on the bed, next to a couple of carrier bags and two £1 coins. He handed me one of each and told me to put them in my pocket. I informed him that I didn't have any pockets and so he snatched both the carrier bag and the pound coin back out of my hands and said he'd give them to me when we got to the pool. I wasn't entirely sure what they were for, but I nodded and smiled politely as usual.

We headed out into the corridor and locked Mike's door behind us. I hadn't brought the key card in from my room, so we would have to make sure we came back together. We opted to use the lift for the first time, since it opened up directly into the entrance to the leisure club below. The hotel was very quiet, even for this time of the morning, causing Mike to check his watch in case he'd misread it. The empty lift arrived almost instantly after we pressed the button, the discomforting quiet of the hotel corridor made me hesitate briefly before getting in. Mike was altogether less phased by this, so he jumped in first and pressed the button for the ground floor.

We walked into the fitness centre reception area and Mike signed us both in to use the facilities. The receptionist gave us two towels and pointed us towards the changing area. Only when we stood in front of the door to the ladies changing area did Mike divide out the towels, carrier bags and £1 coins.

'I'll see you in there, ok?'

'Uhuh.' I replied, before pushing open the heavy door and causing Mike to hastily step a few paces down the corridor towards the men's changing area.

The changing room was empty, that is to say there was nobody else present at that time, but the odd towel and gym bag suggested there was someone, somewhere within the swimming pool complex. I found a small corner that wasn't easily overlooked and took off my t-shirt and leggings. There were lockers in front of me so I opened one and put my shoes and clothes inside. I noticed a slot for the £1 coin I was carrying, so I inserted it and then closed the door and twisted the key to lock it.

I now stood in my bright yellow bikini, with a small key, a round token with a number on it and a large safety pin type device with a plastic covering attaching the two together. I had no idea what I was supposed to do with it, there was almost nowhere on my skimpy costume to affix the key. I was concerned that anywhere I did fasten the safety pin, it would surely dig into me as I swam.

After a minute or two of deliberation, I opened the locker back up, left my belongings in there and pushed the door closed as best I could. There wasn't anything of any value in there, I couldn't imagine somebody would want to steal my dirty t-shirt and leggings.

I stood in front of a mirror in the changing room and was relatively pleased at what was looking back at me – from the neck down anyway. I searched the changing room for an exit that would take me straight to the pool.

I wasn't the strongest swimmer, in fact, I wasn't the strongest anything. To me, swimming was about the feel of the water lapping over my skin and the voyeuristic nature of communal bathing. As I walked out onto the poolside area I scanned my fellow hotel guests, trying to find Mike. As I swept the horizon I saw only a few other people, a middle aged woman and a similarly middle aged man, both with red faces and looking a little out of breath clinging to the side of the pool. At the other end I spotted Mike, so I made my way around the outside of the pool to get in near to him.

I walked cautiously around the damp tiled floor. I had a somewhat irrational fear of slipping at the best of times, but the thought of having to be loaded onto an ambulance in my bikini was a little too much to bear. As such, I walked on the balls of my feet, with my toes pointing upwards slightly, my hands stretched out for balance and with a gait akin to a cartoon villain stalking their prey.

Once I'd made it to the steps I was a little braver, and quickened my pace. The water was surprisingly warm, although not as warm as the ambient temperature of the room might suggest. I waded into the pool and ducked my head under briefly before rising up out of the water, like a Bond girl coming out of the sea – or so I hoped.

Mike greeted me with a reassuring smile, before heading off to swim a couple of lengths while it was quiet. I opted to bob around at one end of the pool and watch him. The middle aged man and woman were at opposite sides of the pool, suggesting to me that they either didn't know each other, or that they were married. The man looked over at me and smiled, politely I thought, then he looked across at the middle aged woman, who looked at him before turning to smile at me. I was no closer to knowing their relationship. I instead focussed on Mike who was now halfway through his return leg and heading towards me. In trying to avoid staring at me, his breaststroke was unusually clumsy and caused him to struggle to keep afloat. He walked the last few yards, since the pool wasn't very deep, before crouching back down into the water next to me.

'There's a Jacuzzi bit there if you want to go in it?' he said.

'Yeah ok.' I replied, unsure of what else to say. I was slightly reluctant to have jets of water firing into me, since I bruised easily.

Mike and I swam and waded respectively, through a little gap in the side of the pool, into a smaller square area, before Mike pushed a button on the side to start the jets. At first nothing happened, then it coughed and spluttered into life in a rather disconcerting way. It seemed like it was going to explode as the pressure built up, but instead, after 30 seconds or so, the jets all burst into life at the same time and the Jacuzzi was in full swing.

I was right to be worried, no matter where I moved the jets seemed to find me and batter me relentlessly. Mike sat right in front of a jet and suggested I do the same, allowing the water to hit the small of my back instead of my sides. This was indeed blessed relief and for a moment I actually started to enjoy it.

'So what do you want to do today?' shouted Mike over the noise of the jets.

I opted not to shout my response, instead I mouthed 'I don't mind' and made a corresponding facial expression. Aware that he'd embarrassed me, Mike chose not to keep shouting, so he nodded, mouthed 'ok' and waited until the Jacuzzi jets turned off before continuing the conversation.

'We can just take it easy, see where the day takes us.' suggested Mike.

'Yeah, sounds good to me, I'm a bit tired after yesterday' I replied.

I stood up from the Jacuzzi and could see Mike looking directly at my chest, which was a little strange as he usually avoided any awkward glances in my direction. It was especially unusual given that I was in my bikini and he'd not wanted to look directly at me moments ago as he swam towards me. I milked the moment for all it was worth, looking up over him, tilting my head back slightly and wringing out some of the water from my hair, sending it cascading down my back. As I returned my gaze to meet his, he had moved from looking at my chest to looking at my midriff, or possibly lower.

'Where did you put your key?' he asked with a sense of urgency, looking back up at my eyes.

Of course, he hadn't been studying my body as I'd assumed, he was just looking for the safety pin with the token and key. I was a little disappointed, but at least he'd been comfortable enough to have a good look for it. I resisted the temptation to turn around and let him check for it on the rear.

'I couldn't find anywhere to pin it on this,' I replied, 'so I just left it in the locker. There's nothing valuable in there so I'm sure it'll be ok.'

'Ah ok, sorry, I just couldn't help noticing it wasn't pinned onto you.' said Mike.

'No need to apologise.' I said, smiling at him and heading back into the pool.

I hoped that he watched me walk away, I even straightened the back of my bikini bottoms by tucking both index fingers just inside the stretchy material and pushing them down over my bum cheeks. I also hoped he knew it was ok to look at me, he didn't have anything to apologise for. I wanted him to know I was more than comfortable with him seeing me like this. I felt that the awkwardness was starting to subside, my actions probably helped in that respect. Is it really voyeurism if the person you're observing is aware and untroubled by the fact that you're looking at them?

I decided to try and swim a width of the pool, opting for a cross between the breaststroke and a doggy paddle, since this was the only way I knew how. I was surprised at just how tiring it was to travel this short distance. As I neared the side wall I was grateful to be able to stretch out and grab the side, one stroke short of a full width. I clung on and caught my breath, just as the middle aged man made his way behind me on another length of the pool.

I waited for the sound of him passing me in the other direction but it never came. I turned round and saw that he was waiting at this end of the pool, a few feet away from me. He smiled again and made small talk, something about him and his wife in London for the weekend, going to the theatre tonight, that sort of thing. I think he wanted me to explain what I was doing in London with Mike, but I didn't. It was far too complicated and frankly I wasn't sure I knew anyway.

Luckily, Mike made his way over and interrupted the red-faced man by smiling at him and saying hello. It struck me that simply smiling at someone is the human equivalent of when animals make loud noises to scare away other less dominant males. Of course I couldn't be sure that Mike was displaying ownership of me, or telling the other male to back off, but it felt good to be guarded by him in this way. After some more small talk, the red-faced man continued with his lengths of the pool and would bother us no more.

'They've got a sauna here,' said Mike, 'have you been in one before?'

'Nope, what's it like?' I asked in reply.

'Hot.' said Mike, concisely and without any hint of irony.

'Yeah I kinda guessed that.' I said, before agreeing to give it a go anyway.

I let Mike lead the way around the poolside this time, partly so I could have the enjoyment of watching him walking in front of me, his wet swim shorts clinging to his firm bottom. My concentration on him caused me to slip slightly, only losing my footing for a fleeting millisecond before recovering, but it was enough to make me look away from him and concentrate once again on tippy-toeing around the poolside. Mike reached the sauna way before me, as a result of my fixation on every step, and had to wait for me to arrive before he could open the door, so as to not let the heat out.

When he was sure I was close enough behind him, he grabbed the wooden handle and wrenched it open forcefully, shepherding me inside the tiny timber-clad room first, before following me in and closing the door quickly behind him. When he turned around I was still standing up, not sure of where to go in a room no bigger than the average en-suite toilet. Mike recommended I sit on the bottom row and so I sheepishly lowered myself onto the dry, pale wooden bench. The room was hot for sure, but not as bad as I'd expected, or so I thought until I touched the wood. The bench was so dry and hot that it pinched the skin on my bottom and forced me to raise up off it momentarily before settling back down.

I sat motionless for a moment, acclimatising to the heat and allowing my lungs to breathe in the warm air. Mike sat above and to the side of me, on the top row, his feet resting on the bench next to me. I leaned back and got another nasty surprise as my back hit the wood behind me, this felt even hotter, if that was possible, but after shifting to and fro a little, I was finally able to lean back and relax. Having come straight from the pool there was a slight liquid barrier between my skin and the heat of the sauna, but it wasn't long before the excess water had dried off. My skin was now bone dry, except for the areas enclosed by my bikini which still held on to some moisture.

I tilted my head to one side slightly and looked at Mike's feet. I had never really looked at them before, not that I ever had cause to, but I wasn't going to pass up the opportunity to study them in more detail. They were quite big, I guessed about two or three sizes bigger than my father's, whose shoes I'd seen by the door and were not much bigger than mine. They were also quite symmetrical, a little muscular looking and somewhat hairy. They were, of course, to me, the most wonderful feet in the world, matted hair finish and all, since they belonged to the object of my affections.

I turned my attention to his ankles, which looked, unsurprisingly, like everyone else's I'd ever seen, including mine. The ankles must be one of the most featureless parts of the human body, I pondered. One could line up a few dozen and most people wouldn't be able to tell male from female, let alone pick out individual people. I stopped looking at his ankles and decided I dare not venture further up the leg since my head and neck position would make it obvious I was no longer casually resting.

I stared forward out of the glass door and saw the middle aged man and middle aged woman engaged in deep conversation. '*Ah, so they are married.*' I thought, either that or Mrs red-faced man was going to walk in shortly and give him what for. As I gazed out, I realised my skin was no longer as dry as it was before, the excess pool water now replaced by tiny beads of sweat. They didn't form large enough to drip anywhere, just enough to secrete from the skin and make it clammy.

No sooner had I deduced this, then I felt larger beads caught up the hairs on the back of my neck. These beads did indeed begin to roll down my back and despite the lack of any discernible smell, I decided they were a sign that I should leave the sauna. I turned around to Mike, who was sweating a lot more heavily than me, and suggested we get back into the pool. He climbed down off the top bench and insisted on opening the door for me. '*What a gentleman*', I thought, before accidentally putting my hand against the scorching glass on my way out and realising why he'd done so.

'We need to grab a shower before we go back into the pool.' said Mike.

'Do we?' I asked, somewhat confused.

'Yeah, it says so on the sign, look.' he said, pointing to an A4 placard by the sauna door.

I didn't bother to read it, I just followed Mike to a large area with a huge vertical shower head hanging above it. He motioned me under it and then reached over and pressed a button on the wall, causing a cascade of fine, cool water to rain down onto me.

Mike then stepped in next to me, extremely close, to shower off some of the sweat from his back and chest. I could barely contain my excitement at his proximity, but I found myself unable even to touch my hands to my body in order to shower properly with him standing so close. I let the water run down me and stood completely still until he'd stepped back out and was walking towards the pool. Once again my mind was alive with sexual thoughts and feelings. Nothing new, but this was certainly one of those experiences I would remember, although my memory might play tricks on me and conveniently omit the swimwear from the recalled image.

We didn't stay in the pool for long the second time round. After a short dip and a length from Mike, it was time for me to get out, change and head back up to the room. We were both pretty hungry having worked up an appetite in the pool. We headed to our respective changing rooms and as I opened the door to mine I noticed it was a little busier than before, a few women in their twenties were changing into Lycra gym outfits. I made my way over to my locker and was pleased to find that my towel and clothes were all still there. I suddenly felt a little self-conscious and opted to take my things into a shower stall to get dressed. I dried myself off, put my bikini into the carrier bag and tied the bag at the top.

I suddenly realised I'd forgotten to bring any underwear with me so I struggled into my leggings and t-shirt and walked back out to the locker area.

I had thought I was being so clever putting my bikini on under my clothes to save time, but now it was wet and in a carrier bag and I had nothing but a pair of leggings and a baggy t-shirt on. Ordinarily I didn't really have to worry about a bra, but walking out from the warm pool area to the air conditioned lifts might cause a problem, or more specifically, two problems. I studied the contents of my locker for a solution but none presented itself. I picked up my carrier bag with the wet bikini and my towel, which I disposed of in the marked bin, before heading out to reception to meet Mike.

Luckily, when I arrived, he was already there, so we walked straight over to the lift and pressed the button. After an interminably long wait, during which

I was holding my t-shirt away from my body in order to disguise the shapes underneath, the lift arrived. We stepped into what was fortunately for me an empty lift and Mike pressed the button for the second floor.

It was at this point that I decided I had nothing to be ashamed of and that I might in fact benefit from pushing the boundaries of our relationship a little further. I let go of my t-shirt and let it fall against my chest. As it did so, the sensation of it touching my nipples, combined with the cool air conditioning, ensured that the shape of them was visible through the t-shirt. I took it further and put my hands behind my back and leant against the side of the lift.

Now the entire shape of my breasts could be made out through my t-shirt and I stood proudly displaying them, looking over at Mike, daring him to turn round. I thought I saw his eyes shift sideways in his head at one point, though it remained facing forward throughout. I was convinced he'd spotted them in his peripheral vision, if only for a brief moment.

The lift reached the second floor and I marched out confidently in front of him, satisfied with myself and in the firm belief that I was slowly winning him over. We reached Mike's room and I turned again to face him as he put his key card in and unlocked the door. I followed him in and made my way over to the adjoining door. I grabbed at the handle and it didn't move. I turned the small silver lock and tried again. Still nothing. It was then that I span round and realised Mike's room had been cleaned, as presumably had mine. The cleaners must have locked the adjoining door from both sides, but I didn't have my key card.

'Er, Mike.' I said, calmly, trying not to panic him, 'They've locked the door and I don't have my key card.'

Mike tried the door again, locking it and unlocking it a couple of times to no avail, before he picked up the telephone and rang down to reception.

After a heated conversation with the receptionist, who was initially unhelpful, he put the phone down and told me we'd have to go down to reception and they'd print another key card for my room. I asked if it was absolutely necessary for me to go too and with a faintly audible sigh Mike headed down to reception on his own.

Chapter 14

I perched myself on the end of Mike's freshly-made bed, keen not to mess up the sheets. I felt so much better for having had a brief swim, it was every bit as cleansing as I'd hoped. I allowed my eyes to close and just sat and enjoyed the silence, along with the smell of my damp hair.

My meditations were soon interrupted by the shrill sound of a mobile phone ringtone. I leapt up and walked over towards the desk where I found Mike's phone. I looked down at the screen and read the name Pete. I don't know what I had planned on doing once I'd got to the phone, I certainly wasn't going to answer it, especially as I didn't know who Pete was. It then occurred to me I didn't really know anyone Mike knew, friends, family, colleagues – no-one.

I sat back down on the bed after I'd stared the phone into submission and the ringing had ended. I thought again about the fact that I rarely heard Mike talk about anyone else. We always talked about my mum – obviously that's how we first came to know each other – but he must have had other friends, he was a pretty likeable fella after all, I certainly thought so anyway.

As I was deep in thought, the likeable fella re-entered and handed me a new key card for my room. I thanked him and walked back out to the hall to let myself back into my room. As I did so, I remembered the phone call and notified Mike that Pete had rung, but that I hadn't answered it. Mike looked slightly bemused at the fact I feigned knowledge of this Pete character, he obviously couldn't recall mentioning him before.

'Oh yes, he's heading off on holiday today, I'd completely forgotten.' said Mike, before striding over to the desk to get his phone.

I left him to it, unlocked my door and entered my room again. My bed too was freshly made and the cleaner had even folded up some of my discarded clothes and underwear onto a chair. *'Third time now'* I thought to myself, before flopping down on the bed.

No sooner had I lay there then my stomach rumbled and I was reminded of my intense hunger. I headed over to the adjoining door and pressed my ear against it. I couldn't tell where Mike was or whether he was busy so I headed for a quick shower to get the chlorine out of my hair, then got dressed for breakfast in my jeans and a clean t-shirt.

I knocked on the adjoining door, unlocked it and let myself into Mike's room. He was sat in the chair by the desk with his phone in his hand typing away. He seemed deep in concentration, so I quietly walked over and perched myself once again on the end of the bed. He finished his typing, which had quickened in pace since my entrance, before forcefully plonking the phone back down and spinning around in his chair.

'Shall we go and get breakfast then? I'll tell you what Pete's voicemail said.'

I nodded in agreement and we headed out of Mike's room to the corridor. This time I had both my key cards in my jeans pocket. I was mildly excited at the prospect of Mike sharing the contents of his voicemail with me. Not least to find out who Pete was, how he and Mike knew each other, that sort of thing. I walked more briskly than usual down the hallway towards the staircase, leading Mike to assume that I was particularly hungry, which I was, but really I just didn't like being kept in suspense.

We walked into the restaurant and were shown to our table. Despite this only being our second morning in the hotel we already had a well-rehearsed routine. Mike went to get one tea and one coffee, I went for two orange juices, then we returned to the table to set them down before heading off in different directions again. This time I returned with scrambled eggs, a little smoked salmon, and two slices of toast. Mike came back with a large bowl of cereal and two apples. In perfect synchronicity we shuffled plates, cups and glasses around the table until we each had our own breakfast in front of us. I slurped at my orange juice and picked up my knife and fork to tuck into my eggs.

'So, Pete's voicemail?' I enquired.

'Right.' said Mike, 'Well, Pete's an old school friend, we don't see each other much these days. We keep in touch though and usually manage to catch up properly once or twice a year. Anyway, he's off on holiday, as I said, so he's just letting me know where he's going, in case of emergency. Also, as I'm not working at the moment, he suggested I pop round to his house at some point as it's empty, for a change of scenery.

'Oh right,' I said, 'how long's he away for?'

'Only a fortnight.' said Mike.

'So are you gonna pop round at some point to check on the house?'

'Well that brings me nicely to my next point,' said Mike, 'I was going to see whether you fancied heading up there with me today?'

I paused, midway through a bite of scrambled egg on toast, to reply.

'Well I guess we could, yeah.' I said uneasily.

'I'm not really selling it am I?' said Mike, 'Pete and his wife live in a lovely old house called 'Ivy Cottage' in a quaint little village in Norfolk. It's a nice place, out in the countryside, fresh air, peaceful... I think you'd like it.'

I recapped the description in my head, old cottage, quaint village, fresh air, quiet. I embellished the description slightly in my head with roaring log fires, plush fur rugs, vaulted beamed ceilings. It sounded lovely, quite romantic too, the perfect setting to get to know Mike better and vice versa.

'It does sound nice,' I eventually replied, 'as long as it's ok for me to go too?'

'Yeah I'm sure Pete won't mind, they've got a spare room that I usually stay in.' said Mike. 'You might have to text your friend and get her to cover for you with your father.'

'Oh yeah, of course.' I replied, firmly in the knowledge that I couldn't do that, as I didn't have the correct phone with me. I'd have to just pretend that I'd okayed it with Lucy and my father. It shouldn't be a problem really, I was perfectly safe and I doubted my father had even noticed I wasn't there.

I rushed through the rest of my breakfast excitedly, downed a still scaldingly hot cup of tea and pushed my plate a few inches away from me to signal that I was done. I then looked up and noticed that Mike was still wading through the giant bowl of cereal and realised that I wasn't going anywhere anytime soon. I decided to use the opportunity to ask some additional questions and find out more about Pete, and therefore Mike, at the same time.

'So tell me more about you and Pete, were you a couple of tearaways?' I asked joshingly.

'Hah,' snorted Mike, 'no not really. We actually weren't friends at first, we were in the same year but in different form groups. We didn't really know each other until sixth form, where we befriended each other in rather unlikely circumstances.'

'Ok, I'm intrigued, go on...' I instructed.

Mike suddenly looked slightly embarrassed and his cheeks went a beautiful rosy red.

I stared directly at him and raised both my eyebrows to encourage him to continue the story.

'Well,' said Mike, 'we both liked the same girl in our school. We were sat next to each other in the lunch room one day. I was looking over at this girl, daydreaming really, when I felt a tap on my shoulder, it was Pete. He sat down next to me and we had a rather frank discussion about the object of our affections. It was all very silly really, two lads just talking about things they knew nothing about. Neither of us would have the courage to ask her out back then, and anyway, to do so would have jeopardised our new-found friendship.'

'Awww that's quite sweet really.' I replied.

'You wouldn't have said that if you'd heard Pete talking.' said Mike, laughing to himself as he picked up his coffee.

I allowed myself to imagine the sorts of things they might have said about the poor girl and shuddered slightly. It also caused me to imagine Mike as a teenager, which was especially weird to me.

'So what was this girl's name?' I asked, 'Did you ever get round to asking her out?'

'Oh I erm, I can't remember her name. That wasn't really the point of the story.' said Mike, 'Come on, let's head up to the rooms and start packing before we miss our check-out time.'

He drank the last of his coffee and stood up immediately, leading me to follow suit. I realised that was to be the end of that conversation. It seemed to have finished rather abruptly, which felt a little strange to me. As we walked back through the reception area I wondered if there was more to that story than Mike was letting on.

I packed my suitcase and backpack, more neatly this time, before knocking on the adjoining door and sitting back down on the end of my bed. Mike entered and wandered around silently, checking behind the curtains, under the bed and around the bathroom to make sure I hadn't left anything. Once he was satisfied, he suggested I come into his room so we could lock my room up and mentally check it off as done.

Mike had packed his bag, but left out all the essentials for the next part of the journey, road map, travel sweets, his mobile phone etc. He passed me the map and the sweets to hold onto while he picked up our bags and walked towards the door. He turned round to survey the scene one more time and then motioned me out the door and into the hallway. We headed down to reception to check out and a porter took our bags to the car and brought it around to the entrance for us.

As we made our way through the large automatic glass doors, two men, different from the previous day but with identical jackets, opened up the doors of the car for us. To my horror one opened up the driver's door and the other the rear passenger-side door.

As I made my way around the car I didn't know how best to deal with the situation. I didn't want to offend the guy but there was no way I was sitting in the back for the whole journey. I stood patiently in front of him, the other side of the open rear door, hoping he'd understand. Alas I found myself having to tell him I was going to sit in the front, at which point he apologised to me with a curt "Sorry, Miss," before shutting it and opening the front door.

Of course Mike found the whole thing very amusing. He wanted me to sit in the front as much as I did, mainly so he didn't have to crane his neck as far to keep an eye on me. Plus we both remembered what had happened last time I was in the back of the car and he'd had to look round to make sure I was ok.

After repositioning his seat, as the porter had rudely altered it, Mike and I were finally on our way to our romantic country retreat.

Chapter 15

Mike told me he 'pretty much' knew the way, as he'd been multiple times before, but suggested I find the page in the road map and familiarise myself with the route in case he needed help. I had never studied a map before, I never really had cause to, so it was harder than I anticipated to find where we were going. Once I'd zeroed in on it, I'd completely lost where London was, so in essence my help proved rather useless. I was no clearer on the route we were taking, but I hoped Mike's confidence in knowing the way wasn't amiss.

As we made our way through the cramped and crowded streets of central London, I felt more eager than ever to get away from the chaos to somewhere more tranquil. I dare not speak to Mike as he battled his way through other cars, aggressive taxis and buses, and an abnormal number of pedestrians who were hell bent on walking out in front of the traffic. It occurred to me that only yesterday, I was one of those pedestrians shouting at the cars as they inched towards my legs while I crossed. Today the roles were reversed and I did feel a twinge of sympathy for them as I stared scornfully in their direction.

It wasn't long before we could see signposts for the M25, a road I'd only ever heard of in the context of ten mile tailbacks. Luckily, I was pretty confident we weren't going on the motorway, my map reading skills suggested we would simply cross under it or over it at some point on our way to East Anglia.

Unfortunately my optimism was short lived as by the time we were within five miles of the junction for the M25 the traffic had ground to a halt anyway.

I took this opportunity to chat to Mike. The anticipation of our romantic country cottage getaway was proving too much for me to bear, so I had to spoil the surprise by finding out as many details as I could before we got there.

'So tell me more about this cottage?' I asked.

'Oh, well, what would you like to know?' replied Mike.

'Does it have a real fireplace with a log fire? Does it have big wooden beams and vaulted ceilings? Does it have a garden? If it does, does it have a pond or a little stream running through it?' I reeled off uncontrollably.

'Ok, ok, one question at a time.' Mike interjected. 'Yes it has a fireplace, we might have to buy wood though. It has a garden, not sure about a pond or a stream, I haven't noticed. Yes it has exposed beams in some of the rooms. I'm kind of surprised you're interested in some of those things though'

'I'm just excited about seeing it, my friends all live in townhouses, like my father's place and my old house, nobody has anything as nice as a cottage.' I replied.

'Ah, well I hope you like it when you see it, and that it's to your taste.' said Mike smirking.

'Don't mock me,' I responded, 'I've lived a sheltered life, I've never seen exposed beams.'

'Haha ok.' replied Mike, still smirking.

'So what are we gonna do when we get there? I mean, what is there to do?'

'Well, we usually just go for walks, sometimes to the local pub, sometimes for a picnic. We tend to just relax and keep things relatively unplanned.' replied Mike.

'A romantic walk sounds nice.' I said.

Then it hit me, I'd actually said the words 'romantic walk' out loud, prior to this I'd thought about phrases like romantic getaway, romantic walk, romantic dinner, but until now they were always part of my internal monologue. I panicked momentarily, unsure of what his reaction would be. As I sat there I could feel time passing by slowly, the ticking of an imaginary clock in my head telling me I'd left it too late to turn it into a joke.

I looked round at Mike, unable to think of anything else to say, or do, in defence. I stared blankly at the side of his head as he looked at the traffic which was slowly moving in front. I gave a nervous smile in his direction, unsure as to whether he would see it or not as he remained looking forward.

'I'm sure we can go for a nice walk.' he replied, smiling back at me.

'*Wow*', I thought, '*was it really as easy as that? Was it as simple as just asking?*' Perhaps I'd been playing it too cool by just trying to get him to notice me. Maybe all this time he'd been thinking the same things I had, romantic dinners, romantic getaways, romantic walks. Maybe he'd been unsure about how I felt about him and he too was looking for some kind of sign.

Or maybe I was reading too much into his response. He hadn't used the phrase *romantic walk*, he'd used the phrase *nice walk*. You'd go for a *nice walk* with your parents, you'd go for a *nice walk* with the dog, heck, you could go for a *nice walk* on your own. I stared back at the map which was open on my lap and considered which of these two scenarios was more likely. Before long I had got lost in a daydream and wasn't really thinking analytically about either possibility.

A car horn brought me to my senses and also signified that we were moving more freely in the traffic now, as everyone seemed to want to swap lanes in order to get to their desired destinations. We crossed the M25 junction and headed off on the main road towards East Anglia. This part of the journey was pretty straightforward – the map told me – we would stay on this road for a while until we were much closer to the village.

I decided the silence had gone on long enough, so I shattered it by turning on the radio.

I left it on the first station I found this time, I wasn't that worried about what music came on, I just wanted a distraction from my own thoughts. I let the sound of soul, swing and 60's pop wash over me. I didn't listen to any of the words, I wasn't moved by any of the rhythms, I just let them fill my senses and shut down my brain to the point of moroseness.

An hour or so passed like this before Mike became concerned at my lack of... well... anything.

'Shall we stop at the next services to stretch our legs and grab a cup of tea?' he asked.

It took me a few seconds to compute that he was talking to me. I took my brain out of standby and replayed the words in my head, in order to understand the question.

'Yeah ok, I could do with a wee as well.' I responded.

I have no idea why I said that. That was the biggest problem with shutting your brain off, when you wake it up, it falsely allows you to think that it's running at full capacity. Many a stupid thing is said when you're half-awake, or half-asleep. I shuddered slightly at my own stupidity. I'm sure Mike didn't want to know that I needed a wee, but he knew nevertheless. It sounded like the sort of thing a kid would say, 'Daddy, Daddy, can we stop? I need a wee!'. I was angry at my own brain and mouth for conspiring to embarrass me in that way.

I needn't have beat myself up so much though as Mike then shared his desire to stop for one too. I definitely didn't need to know that, but I was now glad that I wasn't the only one who'd said it. We pulled into the service station after a few more miles and looked for a parking space as close to the doors as possible. Eventually we settled on one halfway across the car park as the need to go to the toilet outweighed the need to painstakingly search for the empty space nearest the entrance.

As we parked up, I let Mike put away his valuables while I headed straight across the car park with an enforced spring in my step. Finding the toilets was easy, as the flow of foot traffic created two distinct lanes of people either shuffling awkwardly towards them, or strolling confidently away from them, fully relieved. I was soon moving from the first to the second of these lanes and having not seen Mike at any point, I decided to visit the little shop instead.

The array of good for sale at the service station shop was truly baffling. Sure there were travel sweets, magazines, road maps and a plethora of snacks and drinks, but they also seemed to sell gifts, clothing, luggage and electrical goods too. Some of those items seemed to have the most tenuous link to travelling, but I found myself browsing the clothes and portable music players regardless. It wasn't long before Mike found me and suggested we find somewhere for a tea or coffee.

We sat in a little corner cafe, very close to the wafting smell of the fast food outlets just a partition wall away. I happily moved my tea bag up and down in the cup, spinning it left and right as I did so, before eventually mashing it with my plastic spoon in order to turn the tea a more acceptable colour. Mike's filter coffee was similarly pale for some reason, but beggars can't be choosers. It was good to be out of the car and opposite each other, rather than facing forward and talking at the windscreen.

'How far have we got to go?' I asked.

'Only about an hour now I think.' Mike replied. 'We'll skip lunch so we get there quicker.'

'Sure,' I replied, 'I'm not that hungry anyway after our late breakfast.'

'We might have to head out and buy some food at some point as I doubt they've left much in the house while they're on holiday.' said Mike.

I agreed it was unlikely we'd find a feast waiting for us when we got there, but at least if we went shopping I could guarantee finding something I'd like to eat.

'Maybe we can get some picnic food as well if we do?' I suggested.

'Yeah we certainly can, if you fancy a picnic? Weather permitting.' Mike replied.

We turned our heads simultaneously towards the window, having not been particularly aware of the weather until now. It wasn't raining but the sky was an ominous shade of grey, certainly not picnic weather today. It had been relatively bright and warm in London but I worried the best of the weather was behind us now. The British Summer had a habit of being short, but just three days this year would be particularly galling.

We finished our hot drinks and sat for a while, just staring at the moving traffic from our vantage point by the window. The sky grew darker and darker, leading us to make a bit of a dash to the car in the hopes of beating the rain to our destination. We set off swiftly and did indeed manage to keep the greyest of clouds behind us as we continued up the dual carriageway towards our turn off.

'I think it's this one coming up, junction twelve.' said Mike.

'Yep, junction twelve.' I replied, now confident in my map reading and co-piloting abilities.

As we pulled off the main road to a roundabout, Mike insisted he knew the way from this point from memory. I closed the map, but left it in the foot-well with the page marked, just in case. The further we drove the more unusual the place names on road signs became, a sure sign we were headed for a remote location. I read all the hyphenated names out loud for some reason.

'Chorlton-cum-brook'

'Abbey-upon-trow'

'Beckle-by-bough'

'Are you checking these off as we go past them on the map?' asked Mike.

'No I just like saying them out loud.' I replied.

I decided not to announce any more place names. I could tell Mike was having to concentrate harder as we got closer and frankly I was even beginning to annoy myself with it.

Finally we saw a sign for the village we wanted and turned down the even smaller and windier road towards it. As we tip-toed our way down the road, figuratively speaking, we passed a few ramblers literally tip-toeing on the grass verge as we passed. They gave us a wave and I waved back, I felt somewhat compelled to, despite there being no specific social convention I was aware of that deemed it absolutely necessary.

Eventually we'd passed through the village proper, complete with post office, local pub and farm shop. We headed out the other side for half a mile or so up a small hill, until Mike recognised a particular hedgerow and swung the car wildly into a driveway on the left. The violence of the manoeuvre caused me to lurch towards Mike and have to put my hands out to steady myself against his shoulder. This also had the knock-on effect of ruining the first image I got of our holiday home for the next few days, because I was forced to view it side on with my head tilted.

'Sorry about that,' said Mike, 'I thought I was going to miss the turning.'

'So did I,' I replied, 'even as you were making it.'

Once the car had come to a stop and I'd composed myself, I was finally able to absorb the view of the beautiful cottage in front of me.

Either side of the gravel driveway were little patches of lawn, themselves surrounded by a variety of colourful plants and flowers. The path led the eye towards an imposing wooden door, with wrought iron bolts and straps, which sat flush in the middle of the double-fronted stone building. The walls of the cottage were white-washed, but only flashes of white could be seen between the leaves of creeping ivy which covered the majority of the facade.

The mature trees at the front of the garden caused the approach to the cottage to be overwhelmingly dark, with only dappled light piercing the canopies and throwing shards of brightness against the occasional bare white patch of wall.

I opened the passenger side door and stepped out onto the gravel to the sound of a satisfying crunch underfoot. Closing the car door behind me, I span round to see Mike heading around the front of the car towards the house. I shouted for him to wait as I wanted to get the first look, forgetting, of course, that Mike had been here numerous times before. Still, I wanted to *feel* like I was getting the first look.

Mike checked under a flowerpot and found a small brass key and a larger silver coloured one. He wrestled with the locks and bolts on the door until it finally eased open after a swift shoulder charge. He motioned for me to go and have a look around while he got the luggage out of the boot. I didn't need telling twice and excitedly leapt through the large wooden door before it had a chance to fully open.

Chapter 16

Beneath my feet was a hard, stone floor, somewhat uneven. The fact that the entrance hallway was dimly lit, by what little light made it through the front door, caused me to stop dead in my tracks for a moment while my eyes adjusted sufficiently to find a switch. Once I had partially illuminated the area in a soft yellowish glow I could see all the way up to the high vaulted ceiling and, in the space in front of me, the dark shapes of doors leading off to a multitude of rooms waiting for my exploration, which I set about doing immediately after kicking off my shoes.

For a brief time I forgot that this was someone's house I was striding through. It wasn't until I'd opened a door to a small en-suite bathroom, complete with toiletries, that I remembered my role as somewhat uninvited guest, and continued my journey a little more sedately and respectfully.

The bedroom I had wandered into was quite large, with a huge bed, topped with pillows and cushions that had been laid out meticulously. There was one window looking out into the back garden, whilst the other side afforded a view of Mike struggling with our bags from the car boot. I smiled and waved at him through the window, then realised I was probably making things worse by waving, so I went to help.

As I reached the entrance hall again I was just in time to see Mike close the door behind him, having brought in the final few bags by this point. As he did so the house darkened slightly, causing us to scramble around looking for more light switches. One switch turned on some additional spot-lights which were much brighter than the yellowish candle bulbs on the walls.

I could now see what looked to be the kitchen, directly ahead of me and offered to put the kettle on for a cup of tea. The hard stone floor continued through into the kitchen and by now, was beginning to become uncomfortable on my heels and the balls of my feet. I opted to slide across the polished stone floor in my trainer socks so as to give my feet a break.

Finding things in someone else's house is a tricky task, one that makes you realise just how much humans are creatures of habit. Locating the kettle was no problem, but you'd think the tea and coffee would be somewhere nearby. They weren't. A full ten minutes later and with every cupboard open and its contents exposed, Mike wandered in to see what the hold-up was.

The kettle had been boiled so long ago it had stopped steaming altogether, causing Mike to press his hand against it before recoiling and swearing profusely. I informed him that working the kettle was straightforward enough, it was locating the tea that was proving difficult.

After running his hand under cold water for a few seconds – more for show than out of medical need I suspected – Mike grabbed an ornate little box on the windowsill and handed it to me. Inside were two chambers filled with tea bags, they seemed slightly out of place enshrouded in the decorative box. I grabbed two out, popped them into the mugs I'd found and re-boiled the kettle. Knowing Mike would likely pop round, Pete and Carol had left two pints of milk in the fridge, but little else. I finished off making the tea and followed Mike into the living room.

I sat on the large brown leather sofa in the centre of the room and Mike perched next to me. I found myself staring out of a set of patio doors into the back garden, which was bright and colourful in comparison to the front of the house. Small birds could be heard chirping in the trees, the occasional fleeting glance of one darting past the window caused me to stare more intently. Normally I would make a grab for the remote control when entering a living room, but I was happy sitting in near silence and watching the nature documentary unfolding before my eyes.

I sipped at my tea, which was of a drinkable temperature a little earlier than I had expected. As I felt the relative heat of the contents of my cup on the back of my throat I let out an audible shiver. The room we were in now suddenly felt cold, in a manner that tricks your brain into thinking the temperature has dropped sharply. More likely we had been sitting for a few minutes and the residual heat of my running around exploring and Mike's bringing in the luggage had dissipated, causing us to both realise just how cold it was throughout the house.

'Can we put the heating on?' I asked politely.

'Well there's no central heating in an old cottage like this, it's storage heaters and fireplaces only.' came Mike's reply. 'Let's get our luggage into the right rooms, see if there's any food in the house or whether we have to find a supermarket, then we can get a fire going and put the heaters on low in the bedrooms.'

I nodded in agreement and continued sipping and gulping my tea as it cooled further. I took my empty cup back into the kitchen and popped it on the side by the sink. I then wandered into the hallway and grabbed my bags. Mike suggested I have the guest bedroom which was to the back left, just off the kitchen and next to the utility room, while he would sleep in Pete and Carol's bedroom, with the en-suite that I'd stumbled into earlier.

I made my way around to the back of the house – an area I hadn't explored on my initial tour – and pushed open the door to my sleeping quarters. It was a bright and airy room, larger than mine at home, but a little sparsely furnished. There was a small double bed, a single wardrobe, a chest of drawers and a little side table by the bed with an alarm clock on.

The room was extraordinarily cold, more so than the living room or the kitchen. I walked around to the heater affixed to the wall by the window and placed my hand against it. The cold metal met my skin and for a moment felt warm, then latterly icy cold. I searched frantically for a way to turn this contraption on, but it wasn't obvious, then I remembered Mike saying we should wait, in case we had to go out for food.

I made my way back out and into the kitchen to wait for Mike who arrived shortly after to search for dinner. I did enquire as to whether it was ok to eat their food but Mike insisted it would be fine, as long as we replaced it, we'd have to find our own after tonight. He stood in front of the open freezer and I kept my distance. For some reason it hadn't occurred to me to go and find a hoodie or something from my bag, instead I just stood, shivering, perhaps hoping for a warm embrace, or at the very least, permission to put some heating on.

'Ok I've found a frozen family-sized lasagne, I'm sure we can have that and we'll just buy another one to replace it when we go shopping tomorrow.' said Mike.

'Does that mean we can have some heat on now?' I asked, shifting the focus from providing nourishment to staving off pneumonia.

'Haha, yeah ok, we can put some heating on, do you know how to work the storage heater in your room?' asked Mike.

'Not really, no.' I replied, eager to make sure it was done properly, as well as to potentially provide the thrill of having him bend over in my room.

I followed Mike into the guest bedroom, jumped onto the bed and sat while he – to my immense disappointment – squatted down beside the storage heater and flicked a switch before adjusting a dial. He informed me that he'd set it to '2', which, I was told, should take the chill off the room by the time I went to bed later. He darted out of my room to go and set the heater in the main bedroom. I didn't stick around to wait for the heat and headed back into the living room, which I was convinced was the warmest place in the house at that time.

This time, upon entering, I scanned the sofa and coffee table for a remote control. None seemed to present themselves and so I started looking a little harder, first under the coffee table, then on the armchairs, before deciding that Pete and Carol must be one of those couples who stupidly replace the remote control each night on top of the television, thus negating the purpose of it being 'remote'.

As I turned round to check, I realised my error immediately. There was, in fact, no television at all. It didn't take me long to realise this once I'd turned round, since there was really nowhere for a television to be. All the chairs pointed towards the fireplace. I felt a little lost and slumped dejectedly into the armchair furthest from the patio doors.

Mike entered, but didn't notice my sullen expression. Instead he marched straight over to the fireplace and began to pile some logs up over some smaller pieces of wood. '*At least a fire might provide some level of entertainment.*' I thought.

Once Mike had created a ramshackle Jenga-like structure, he stepped back for a moment to admire his handiwork, before deciding that he had better try lighting it to get the full effect. He poked in a fire-lighter at the bottom, under the smaller pieces of wood, and lit it with a match. It burned brightly but steadfastly refused to ignite anything around it. It was at this point that I got the entertainment I was missing out on in the absence of television.

Mike knelt down on the floor, at a forty-five degree angle to one side of the fireplace. He then squashed his body down as flat as he could get it, in order to blow air into the kindling crucible he'd created. As he arched his back over his legs his polo shirt rode up his back and his jeans, though pinned to his hips, moved slightly in the opposite direction to reveal the merest hint of his bottom.

I say the merest hint as it's a topic of much debate where the small of the back ends and the top of the bottom begins. Suffice to say there was a slightly dark area, just below the protruding coccyx, which alluded to the parting of the buttocks. It fascinated me greatly and I stared at it as though staring into the void. The sight of this dark area allowed me to visualise the rest of his bottom much more vividly than I had been able to prior to this reveal. As I did so I felt a warmth through my body, for the first time since entering the cold house.

Mike then leapt up from his position and, as luck would have it, my gaze was aimed directly at the fire instead. He would have no idea that my eyes were fixed in that direction before the inferno revealed itself. Sadly I then realised that any warmth I had felt was likely from the now roaring fire, rather than the one that was burning inside me.

As Mike headed into the kitchen to read the instructions on the lasagne box, I found myself completely transfixed by the fire. The warm hues of orange and red twirled and danced against the blackened hearth and sent forth bursts of colour which reflected back off the whitewashed walls of the room. I could see shadows flickering in my peripheral vision but still my gaze was fixed on the harshly bright flames in front of me.

The longer I stared, the more my eyes seemed to dry out, my corneas felt like they were being singed. I couldn't look away though, I felt compelled to keep focused on the flame, regardless of the signals in my brain informing me of the risk. Just before the discomfort became too much to bear, the sight in my peripheral vision of the only other object that held this power over me, began to appear.

'It's really going now isn't it?' came the voice.

I turned and nodded at the blurry pale figure sitting in the other armchair, its edges ill-defined and the colours of its clothes flaring. I closed my eyes tightly shut for a few seconds and shook my head slightly, before reopening them. There sat Mike, with a slightly bewildered look on his face.

'Were you hoping for someone else?' he said.

'No, of course not, why?' I asked.

'You looked like you were closing your eyes and making a wish, that's all.' he replied.

'Maybe I was.' I said, before smiling softly at him.

This just made Mike more confused, so I quickly changed the subject to dinner and our options for entertainment, in light of the lack of television. He informed me that the lasagne would take 45 minutes and so he would put it in the oven at around 6pm. He suggested we eat in the dining room and that we might be able to play a game after dinner if we could find one. It seemed that playing board games was the usual activity when visiting Pete and Carol's house.

Mike reeled off a list of games in vague, nonsensical terms. The one with the plasticine, the one with the coloured pens, the one with the little mirror you had to use to write down your answers. Each sounded more implausible than the last but I guess half the fun for adults playing board games is the ability to revert to a child-like state of confusion and vulnerability.

I reluctantly agreed to this plan, although I hoped to avoid the board games in favour of a more romantic evening at the dinner table. I shifted my gaze back to the fire, which although still producing flames, was decidedly lacklustre compared to its earlier ferocity. It now provided a subtle glow, which periodically pulsated and burnt brighter, before returning to its original colour. Occasional flames ignited and appeared through gaps in the wood, then as soon as they had arrived they were gone.

I liked to imagine the fire was telling a story, with each convulsion of colour and ejaculation of flame reflecting prevalent moments in the narrative. My story, until recently, had been that of the unlit fire, but this weekend, it mirrored the liveliness and unpredictability of the flame.

I had been lost in thought for the best part of an hour by this point, unaware that the sun was fading behind the trees in the garden and the room was now lit, as well as warmed, by the fire I'd been enthralled by. I peered at a small clock on the mantelpiece and realised it was gone 6pm. I looked over at Mike who was lost in a book, one I hadn't even seem him pick up. I asked if it was time to put the lasagne in the oven. He reminded that he'd done it five minutes ago, that he'd asked me if I was hungry and I'd nodded. I had no recollection of this, but as one does I dutifully pretended I remembered, now that he'd said so.

I was hungry, a little tired from travelling too. To be honest I was wishing this evening away as quickly as possible, as I held onto the idea of our romantic walk and picnic for tomorrow. Neither of us had mentioned it again, I certainly didn't want to seem pushy, but I wanted to be sure it was still going ahead and that he hadn't changed his mind. I opted to subtly ask about what the weather might be like for tomorrow, to give me an easy segue into our plans for the day.

'It should be nice enough, we'll head out to the shops in the morning and grab some stuff for the picnic eh?' said Mike.

'Yeah. Definitely.' I replied, struggling to contain my excitement.

I coyly left the room under the pretence of going to the toilet, but really to hide my flushed cheeks. They were red with a mix of excitement, embarrassment, and heat from the fire. I threw cold water over my face and waited patiently for them to return to a paler, more flattering colour. I decided to wash my hands thoroughly for dinner while I was there, and then head into the much cooler bedroom to read my magazine before dinner.

I glanced at an article about bold geometric prints, accompanied by a variety of colourful photographs of impossibly tall models wearing such patterns. The problem with fashion tips in magazines is that unless you're six foot tall the clothes they recommended simply don't work. An above the knee dress was in fact just below the knee for me, a maxi dress dragged along the floor behind me.

I quickly turned to my favourite article – 'Five steps to snag your man.'

"Step Three: Compliment him.

You should pay your man a compliment, guys like receiving them just as much as us girls do. Make it subtle, don't say it repeatedly and don't be too forward. Stick in safe territory, compliment his clothing or his hairstyle, rather than saying his eyes are like two deep blue oceans that you want to dive into."

I thought long and hard about how I could compliment a man who, although I found attractive, had absolutely no sense of style, nor a particularly bold or interesting haircut. The things I liked about him, appearance-wise, were all the things I had seen in stolen glances or accidental encounters. They weren't things I could readily compliment him on. 'Nice arse.' I considered myself saying next time he bent down to stoke the fire.

I decided to refer back to step two, unsure that I had satisfied the portion about making lively and interesting conversation. Perhaps I could have a better attempt at that over dinner that night. I tucked the magazine under my pillow, keeping it on the correct page, before leaping up enthusiastically and making my way to the dining room to wait for our food.

Chapter 17

I was sat at the dining table for a few minutes before Mike even realised I was there. He walked past the doorway initially, on his way to the kitchen, before doubling back and poking his head around the corner. I smiled at him and he carried on to the kitchen, to get cutlery and crockery. I considered that I should probably get up and help, but I was still enjoying the relief of the cool dining room and didn't want to stray into a kitchen, which was sure to be warmed by the oven that had been on for an hour. Instead I waited for Mike to return with the cutlery, before grabbing it off him to demonstrate that, in my own way, I was helping.

I laid out the place settings, first with us sat at the extremities of the oval table. Then, uncomfortable with the distance between us that created, I placed them either side of the middle, so that our legs might – accidentally or otherwise – graze each other's on occasion.

On top of a cabinet over to one side of the room was a candle, so I moved it to the centre of the table and began searching for matches. I assumed that in one of the drawers of the cabinet I would find some, but after a minute or so of sifting through a melee of tape measures, sticky tape, miniature pens and scraps of paper, I was interrupted by Mike, who seemed keen to stop me rifling through his friends' possessions.

After I made clear my intentions, he returned to the kitchen briefly and then back to the dining room with some matches, before lighting the candle and taking them away again. It was moments like that which jolted me back to reality. Perhaps I was being oversensitive but I felt as though he'd specifically lit the candle himself, to avoid me attempting it and inadvertently burning the whole cottage down.

I sat back at the table, with a rather glum expression and decided not to assist with the dinner preparations any further, as a form of protest. I heard the clattering of plates and serving spoons and a mild swear word directed, it seemed, at the oven gloves, which clearly weren't serving their purpose.

I began to feel slightly guilty, but not so guilty that I got up to help. Mike brought in two plates with lasagne positioned oddly to one side. Odd because it wasn't to the side of anything, since he couldn't find any salad or bread to accompany it. The lasagne thus looked a little sad and pathetic, spilling its contents across the empty side of the plate and retaining none of the structural integrity of the picture on the box.

Mike looked at me apologetically, and I, still a little miffed at not being allowed to light the candle, didn't let him off the hook and instead silently tucked into my first bite. Having been disappointed by the aesthetics of the lasagne in comparison with its box, I wondered if the cardboard itself might have tasted better too. The pasta was pretty limp and lifeless, the white sauce coagulated and the meat was somewhat grainy in texture. This lacklustre evening wasn't helping me to forget my troubles back home, nor was it setting the mood for what I hoped would be an enjoyable walk and picnic tomorrow.

'Is everything ok Rebecca? You seem a bit down.'

I raised my head briefly from my dinner and upon seeing his concerned face I relented and engaged in conversation.

'Yeah, I'm ok, sorry. Just thinking about home.'

'Do you want to talk about it?' he enquired.

I realised that when presented with the opportunity to talk a few days ago, I had rejected the offer and hoped for a distraction. The problem with the distraction technique, is that it requires bigger and bigger sacrifices to allow it to continue. It's the reason middle-aged men come home one day with the keys to a convertible sports car. Some middle-aged men anyway, not Mike, for him cleaning his car would be a big step. As we sat around the large dining table eating a flavourless ready-meal, the distractions had all but faded and I felt obliged to deal with the problems back home.

'Ok,' I said, 'just let me finish this.'

I didn't really want to finish my lasagne, but I wanted time to formulate some of my thoughts in my head before blurting them all out. There were a lot of things I'd wanted to say, a lot of feelings that remained unresolved after my Mum had died. I hadn't really talked about them before, but if anyone was going to be able to get it out of me, it was Mike. Mike, my knight in shining armour, the man whose shirt I'd soaked with my tears in that hospital corridor six months ago.

I pushed the floppy pasta and sticky sauce around the plate for another minute or two, at no point brining any of it closer to my mouth. Then I put my knife and fork in the half-past-six position and nudged the plate a few inches into the middle of the table. Mike instantly picked it up and took it into the kitchen before returning with two small bottles of beer he'd found in the fridge.

'Here, this is how we guys talk about stuff like this, with a beer in hand.' said Mike as he offered me one of the bottles.

I took the bottle from him, not really wanting it, but not wanting to seem impolite either. I wasn't sure why he was referring to me as one of the guys, but like a member of the royal family visiting a former island colony and being presented with a strange object, I felt compelled to join in the custom and offered my thanks.

'So tell me what's on your mind?' he asked, in a sympathetic tone.

I didn't really know where to start, but as I began to speak, my thoughts and fears spilled out in a chaotic mess, leaving Mike frantically trying to make sense of a whole host of repressed feelings, pent-up anger and resentment.

'I hate living with my Father.' I started. 'Everything there is different. I feel like an impostor, a guest in his house. We argue constantly, I can't understand why, I never argued with my Mum. If I leave a single item out of place in the kitchen, he screams, but he's allowed to leave stuff all over the worktops and use every teaspoon in the house. I'm constantly treading on eggshells around him, trying not to make noise, trying not to touch anything. The only sanctuary I have is my bedroom, but even that isn't the haven it should be.

'The bed frame itself has come from my bedroom at home, but the mattress is different. It's much firmer and barely buckles when I lay on it, like those thin blue mats you have to do forward rolls on during school PE lessons. It's about as comfortable too. The room is always cold and I hate the cold. I once turned the radiator up to the highest setting and of course my father shouted at me in the morning and told me he couldn't afford the gas bill. He removed the thermostat from the radiator the following day. Still, it was the best night sleep I'd ever had at his house.

'I spend a lot of time out with my friends now, much as I did when I lived with my mum. The difference is I used to spend time with them because I enjoyed it, now I do it more out of the dread of having to go home. On an average week, I spend three nights sleeping over at Lucy's, usually with the excuse that we're going to be working late on a school project. We rarely have that much homework to do and when we do we'd rather spend time just chatting and watching DVD's. I still feel like a guest in Lucy's house, but at least I'm a welcome one.

'The nights I can't stay at Lucy's, I just sit in my bedroom, sometimes not doing anything at all. I have a small portable television but the signal isn't great. I prefer just to sit and think. Sometimes I think about school, my friends, something funny that happened that day. Sometimes I think about my mum, reminisce about holidays, day trips we took, that sort of thing. I've stopped crying when I think about my mum. I cried a lot in the first few weeks, but then one day, I just stopped. I'm still sad, but there's a kind of numbness that surrounds me when I think of her now. I just close my eyes and allow her to fill my thoughts. It doesn't make me happy but it takes the edge off the sadness and the loneliness.

'And there's a lot of loneliness, it's probably the overriding feeling I have on any given day. Even when I'm with my friends at school, or in my father's company, I may not be alone but I still feel lonely. My mum was my best friend, my confidant, she knew everything about me and could always offer advice when I had problems to contend with. Simple, everyday teenage problems. Now those problems go unsolved, or at least undiscussed.

'I miss her hugs too. When everything got too much for me I could always rely on my mum for a hug. I hug my friends at school, but they're only fleeting hello or goodbye hugs. When my mum wrapped me tightly in her arms, sometimes for two or three minutes, I instantly felt better about everything. There's no real affection from my father, that's probably as much my fault as it is his, I just don't really want any physical contact with him. Sometimes he hugs me goodbye, I suspect more out of social convention than anything else.

'Some days I wonder why my mum had to leave me. I know she was ill and things weren't under her control, but they must be under someone's control.

What divine power decided to take my mum from me? What deity, in his or her infinite wisdom, decided that the world would be a better place if I lost my mother? Was it all part of some grand plan for the universe? Cos I can't understand how it can possibly be a good thing. I'm not stronger for having to overcome adversity, I feel weaker.

'Sometimes I even blame my mum. It's a horrible thought and I feel lousy every time it crosses my mind, but still there are days where she bears the brunt of my anger and frustration. She was supposed to protect me, to guide me, to be the one person who looked after me when I was in need. I'm in need now and where is she? Why did she have to leave me with my father, out of all the people who could have cared for me? There must have been a better solution, one that would have ensured both my safety and also my continued happiness.

'Surely my mum had time after her first stroke. We had six months left together. Why didn't she make alternative arrangements during that time? She knew how uncomfortable I felt around my father, I'd rather have been placed in care, or taken in by a nice foster family. Maybe Lucy's mum would have agreed to take me in. Did she even investigate any of those options? I can't believe that she didn't think about me, how I'd feel if I had to go and live with him.

'Sometimes I wonder why this happened to me, whether I'd done something to deserve this. I wonder whether I could have done more around the house, helped out even more than I did. Maybe if I'd just done more, she'd still be here. I thought things were ok, maybe I should have spotted the signs over Christmas. Perhaps if I hadn't been so focused on what presents I wanted and more focused on my mum's condition I'd have seen something. If I could go back and answer the question again I know what I'd say I really wanted for Christmas, instead of a new smartphone.

'I thought I couldn't cope towards the end when she was alive. But I can't cope now she's gone either. Everything feels like a struggle, my schoolwork, my responsibilities at my fathers. I get distracted easily, by everything, not just thoughts of my mum. I can't seem to concentrate at all any more. I feel so lost and helpless.

'And I feel sick all the time, sick to my stomach. Then sometimes I am sick. I don't think there's anything wrong with me, I just can't seem to get rid of the nauseating feeling of being alive, while my mum no longer is.'

At this point – after around ten minutes of pouring my heart out – I just broke down into a babbling mess. No further words made sense through lungs that were fighting for breath and a mouth sticky with saliva and coagulated white sauce.

I realised I still had the bottle of beer in my hand, and brought it to my lips in order to rehydrate myself and wash away the taste in my mouth. I took a large swig and the beer, that seemed to consist solely of bubbles, foamed around the inside of my mouth, the bitter taste doing little to cleanse my palate. I swallowed hard and momentarily stopped crying, allowing me to wipe away the tears from my eyes and look up at Mike.

He seemed lost for words, which was probably just as well as I had produced enough for the both of us. His eyes shifted around in their sockets, as if surveying a landscape in his mind, trying to make sense of the complex narrative that came at him in tumultuous waves. Finally he attained a moment of clarity and opened his mouth to address me.

'Ok, firstly, just listen to me, let me say what I have to say.'

I nodded and took a deep breath to repopulate my lungs with oxygen.

'It's not unusual to be asking questions like that,' he began, 'it's normal to have lots of strange thoughts and feelings when dealing with bereavement. You've been through more than most girls your age and you've been so brave, and your mum would be so proud of you. I understand that you feel let down, even angry at your mum, for not providing you with the love you needed after her first stroke. That's normal. It's ok to feel like that. I know how much you loved... *love*, your mum, and I'm sure she wishes she could be here for you now.

'She couldn't have known what would happen after her stroke, I didn't know either. I was there a lot during that time and neither of us wanted to think the worst. Your mum thought that if she stayed positive, things would be ok. She hadn't really considered what would happen if she became ill again. I'm sure she would be heartbroken to know that you were unhappy now.

'You'll make peace with these things one day, it's just hard right now when you're living with your father. I'll do whatever I can though, to make things easier on you, to give you hope of a normal life.'

He paused briefly before delivering words I would never forget.

'If you don't get the love that you need at home, you'll always have it from me.'

I burst out into tears again, a combination of happiness, sadness and sheer exhaustion. Oddly, on this occasion, Mike didn't come to console me. He just sat the other side of that table and passed me the tissue box from on top of the cabinet. I grabbed a handful of tissues and haphazardly pressed them against my face. Then I grabbed a couple more and meticulously dabbed at the corner of my mouth and eyes, until I resembled something half-human at least. I looked up at him and quietly muttered 'thanks'. Then I headed back to the bathroom to catch my breath and gather my thoughts.

I returned a few minutes later and Mike was still sat at the table, still sipping at his beer, and evidently still wrestling with a multitude of thoughts of his own. I didn't really want to say any more, I was worn out from the emotional stress of relating all this to him. I told him I was going to go and read one of my magazines in bed. He asked if I was sure I was ok to be on my own. I convinced him that I needed specifically to be alone at this time. I forced a half-smile and held it a fraction of a second, which was as long as I could manage, before heading to my room. I grabbed the magazine from under my pillow and opened it at a random page, before getting undressed and into bed.

It didn't take long for me to realise it was still freezing cold in my bedroom. I slipped carefully out of the covers, trying not to disturb them, and crouched down in front of the storage heater with my arms in front of my bare breasts, hiding them from nobody in particular. I reached out the back of my hand and pressed it against the heater. It wasn't as cold as it had been, the cold touch of metal, but it wasn't exactly warm either. It was room temperature, although in a room that's already feeling quite cold I wasn't sure that was an entirely relevant statement. I threw caution to the wind, turned the dial from 2 to 4 and clambered back into bed lest I freeze, or be caught in this uncompromising position.

I tucked the covers around me, like I was the filling in a sausage roll, before returning to my magazine, or more specifically the 'Five steps to snag your man.'

"Step Four: First contact.

Establishing physical contact is important when transitioning from a friendship to a potential relationship. Don't just reach out and make a grab for him or pounce on him when he enters a room though. Try placing a friendly hand on his shoulder, or touching his forearm when he says something amusing."

Mike had put his hand on my shoulder countless times so far this weekend, so maybe I didn't have to worry about overcoming this boundary. I couldn't specifically recall a time when I'd initiated the contact though. In fact I recalled how when we showered together at the pool I was frozen in fear. Perhaps the touching of his forearm when he said something funny might be a good place to start.

I closed my eyes and imagined how that scenario might play out. Strangely – even in my daydream-like state – it didn't end well. I was talking to Mike about something, I grazed his forearm with my fingers and he sat bolt upright, scratched the precise area I had inadvertently tickled and changed the subject. If I couldn't even get it right in my dreams what chance did I have trying it for real?

I felt comfortable, albeit slightly vulnerable, in his presence. I had to gain the upper hand and shift the balance in my favour. I had to make Mike feel vulnerable in some way, then I could be confident and assured and allow myself to touch him.

I kept reading other parts of the magazine until my eyes became heavy. I left it somewhere in the middle of a story of a girl who'd singed her own hair using hair straighteners without a safety mark. I distinctly remember having little sympathy for her before I drifted off to sleep.

Chapter 18

I woke up and checked my phone to see what time it was – 06:23. I turned away, closed my eyes briefly and checked again – 06:24. I eventually accepted that it really was that early in the morning.

It was hard to distinguish time, as the overgrown garden blocked what little light was available, it could have been anywhere between 3am and 9am for all I knew. But it was definitely approaching 6:30am, that I could be sure of. That and the fact it was at least as cold as it was the previous night, if not colder.

I shuffled my body to the edge of the bed, risking the icy blast of the hinterland beyond the covers. I stretched out my foot and pressed it against the storage heater. It took me a second or two to interpret the signals to my brain, it was either hot, or cold, but definitely not room temperature. I left it there momentarily until I'd deciphered the type of discomfort I was feeling and concluded it was indeed cold. What little warmth it had generated last night had now dissipated and it was back to being as cold as it was when we'd arrived in the house.

I wrapped myself firmly in the duvet again and let out a big sigh, which instantly formed a visible breath into the cold air above the bed. I pondered my options for warmth. I could get up, head into the living room and attempt to light a fire. I could go to the bathroom and grab a hot shower or run a bath. Or my preferred option, I could go into Mike's bedroom and snuggle up to him for warmth.

I mentally began re-reading the article from the magazine about making physical contact. I wasn't sure that was what they had in mind. I decided that the fire wasn't a good idea and so I pulled back the covers, quickly threw on a hoodie and my leggings and headed into the bathroom.

It was even colder in the bathroom, perhaps because it had no heater, or possibly because the blue wall tiles made it appear so. I opted for a bath, that would give me maximum warmth, provided there was some hot water, so I ran the hot tap and sat by the side of the bath with my fingers dangling over the edge in anticipation. I periodically waved them from left to right under the stream of water until eventually I was satisfied it was running hot.

I put the plug in and let the scalding water pour freely into the bath, puffing up hot steam as it did. I occasionally dipped a finger in, just to check it my mind wasn't playing tricks on me again. It was a long ten minutes waiting for the bath to fill, during which time I sat on the toilet seat fully clothed allowing the warm water to heat the room around me.

When I was sufficiently warm I took off my hoodie and was about to stand up to take my leggings off when I got distracted by the lines from the sheets that had formed across my body overnight. I found myself tracing them with my finger, across my chest and down my stomach, trying to create a mental dot to dot picture. The lines were a bit too jagged to create anything interesting, but it amused me in my sleep deprived state to try. I noticed the bath getting dangerously full and leapt up to turn the taps off before wrestling off my leggings, turning off the harsh bathroom light and plunging myself into the warm and welcoming bath.

Despite jumping from cold to hot, my body instantaneously covered itself in goose-bumps. It also appeared even paler than usual under the water. Only when I lifted up a leg did the goose-bumps disappear and the true colour of my skin become apparent, it was a bright red hue. The water was only fractionally too hot.

If I kept very still it didn't really burn at all, plus the cold from the night before was a distant memory so I was willing to put up with a little pain. After a few minutes the intense heat died down, leaving me with a perfectly nice bath, my entire body, save for my face, was now submerged in blissful warmth. I realised I had no idea what time it was now, but I was happy not knowing. I closed my eyes and allowed the heat to completely permeate me.

***

The next thing I knew, I was awoken by a sudden shard of light that darted across my partially closed eyelids. In a state of relative confusion I opened my eyes further and as quickly as the light had appeared it had gone. Now all around me was dim again. In addition, the warm sensation had been replaced by a cooler, almost tepid one. I moved my hand around beside me in the bath, it was definitely cooler than it had been when I closed my eyes.

I got out of the bath and began to dry myself off, still pondering this confusing array of lights and temperatures. I towelled off, put on my leggings and jumper and headed out of the bathroom with a small towel wrapped around my head.

The first thing I realised upon heading out of the bathroom was that it was much brighter out there then when I had come in. I got dressed speedily in my still-cold bedroom, throwing on some jeans and a t-shirt under my hoodie, then headed towards the living room where I was met by the sight of Mike pacing up and down by the patio doors.

'I'm sorry Becky.' he said.

My face showed no signs of acceptance of his apology, or for that matter understanding. So he continued.

'I got up and was walking towards the kitchen, when I noticed your bedroom door was open.'

'Ok...' I replied, still none the wiser.

'Well, when I saw you weren't in there, I panicked a bit, especially after our talk last night.'

'Right...' I said, keen for him to hurry up and get to the point.

'Well that's when I saw the bathroom door was closed, but the light didn't seem to be on.'

It suddenly dawned on me the origin of the shard of light that had stirred me from my relaxing slumber.

'So you came in while I was in the bath?' I asked with little intonation to my voice. 'I wondered where the light came from. Sorry, you weren't to know I was in there. My room was really cold when I woke up so I got up and ran myself a bath.'

'Oh ok, let me go and have a look at your storage heater.' he said, darting out of the room.

I sat in one of the armchairs and chuckled to myself. At least that was one barrier that had been unceremoniously torn down. He'd seen me naked now, I figured there was no going back. It really ought to have phased me more than it did. Perhaps I should have appeared more incensed or perturbed by it than I was. Maybe by not being bothered it looked like I wanted him to see me naked, which of course I did – but I didn't want him to know that yet.

Mike returned shortly after, with a deeply apologetic tone of voice. He'd barely got out the words 'I'm sorry...' before I'd cut him off and told him to forget about it. This time, however, he wasn't apologising for walking in on me but rather the temperature in my bedroom. He couldn't work out what was wrong with the heater but apparently it should have got warmer than it did. He guided me into the master bedroom to show me how his heater was set on '2' and the room was noticeably warmer. I nodded in agreement, unsure of how that knowledge was supposed to comfort me.

'You can sleep in that bedroom tonight.' he said, on his way out of the room.

'Where will you sleep?' I asked, with a calm tone that belied the excitement bubbling underneath.

'Well I'll figure something out, I'll see if I can fix that heater or maybe get a fire going and sleep in the living room.' said Mike.

'Oh, ok.' I responded, with a hint of disappointment in my voice that, on this occasion, I was unable to hide.

'Anyway never mind that, I'll go grab a shower and then we'll get some breakfast.' said Mike.

'I'll be sure not to walk in on you!' I shouted after him as he left the room.

I hoped that on some level, while he was showering, he'd think about that very possibility. I knew that every time he told me he was going to grab a shower it filled my head with corresponding images. Perhaps it would be the same for him, especially now 'Shower Mike' had been introduced to 'Bath Becky'. I did consider deliberately walking in on him in the shower, with the pretence that I was getting my own back. I opted instead to remain in the armchair, safe in the knowledge that the thrill of thinking I might walk in on him was sure to trump the act of my actually doing so.

I sat upright in my chair and began to think about the day ahead. We'd settled on a romantic walk and a picnic in the countryside. I had used the word 'romantic' previously and Mike hadn't corrected me so I had no reason to stop using it now.

I stood up and made my way to the patio doors to gauge the weather. The sky was relatively clear, except for the odd fluffy white cloud in the distance.

It seemed like it should be a fine day, despite how cold the old stone-walled cottage got at night.

I headed into my bedroom and delved into my travel suitcase to look for the perfect outfit for such a summer's day. Staring back at me was the dress Mike had bought me in London, brightly coloured, light and airy, with a shape that would flow in the breeze. I hung it up over the door frame and headed back to my armchair in the living room, satisfied with my choice.

I could heard Mike stomping around in the hallway and so I sat patiently, waiting for him to close the door of the master bedroom, before leaping up and striding to the kitchen to put the kettle on. In my mind, the ability to correctly sense when it was time for a cup of tea and then provide one, was an important part of any relationship. My mum had this technique down to a fine art, so I had learnt from the best, and as Mike entered the kitchen I turned around with a freshly made cup and handed it to him.

'Ah you're a star Becky.' said Mike, sipping at the tea before setting it down on the side to look for breakfast. He rummaged in a cupboard, while I leapt up onto the kitchen counter and sat my tea next to me. Various extremely healthy cereals made their way up onto the work top above Mike's head, while he remained hidden by the cupboard doors. Eventually he got up and surveyed in more detail our choices for breakfast. Swedish Muesli, Porridge Oats, High Fibre Flakes and a tub with what appeared to be a proprietary blend of all three.

'I'll try the Swedish Muesli,' I called across the kitchen, 'cos, you know... when in Stockholm.'

Mike smirked at my awful joke and decided he too would opt for the muesli. He poured out two bowls and we took them into the dining room to eat. I always felt like a grown up when eating muesli. Nutritionists had decreed long ago that, for adults, breakfast was a meal to be endured and not enjoyed. I dutifully polished off a variety of hard brown oats and grains with the odd sweetened lingonberry providing precious respite from the dull lifeless taste. This meal was to be my penance for the treats that lay ahead.

Mike cleared up the dishes and left me in charge of writing a shopping list for the picnic. I searched the drawers nearby and found some post-it notes and a biro with which to do so. I wrote down the most popular picnic items I could think of, quiche; cocktail sausages; pork pies; scotch eggs and some cakes. I quickly scrawled 'drinks?' on the bottom of the list in what little space I'd left and handed it to Mike upon his return.

'Oh, ok, if that's what you like.' he replied.

I was a little puzzled by his response. That wasn't a list of my favourite foods, it was a list of traditional picnic foods, I wasn't sure how I could have gone wrong. Not wishing to antagonise him or risk a scene in the supermarket later, I just stuck to my guns and pretended those were my selections for what I wanted to eat. A picnic should be a picnic after all, you can't go getting cutlery out and tucking into duck a l'orange – that's just al fresco dining.

While Mike went looking for where he'd discarded his car keys the previous day, I stayed at the dining room table and debated whether to wear my jeans and jumper to the supermarket or put on my dress. I spent two minutes or so weighing up the pros and cons of each choice before Mike stood in the dining room doorway, proclaiming that he was ready and assuming I was too. Thus my decision was made for me, I slipped on my shoes and headed towards the front door looking somewhat scruffy.

I got into the passenger side of the car and immediately pulled down the sun visor to reveal the little mirror underneath. I looked fleetingly at my reflection and, deciding no good could come of it, instantly returned it to the upright position to pretend I hadn't caught sight of myself. It was a good thing – I thought – that nobody round here knew me. I wouldn't have been seen dead looking like this back home.

Mike jumped in beside me and started the engine, before turning to make sure my seat belt was fastened, then spinning the wheels as he attempted to reverse out of the gravel driveway.

Chapter 19

The nearest supermarket was around eight miles from Ivy Cottage – one of the smaller out-of-town stores that serves the surrounding villages. The drive through the countryside was pleasantly quiet, both inside and outside of the car. Mike was driving far more sensibly, presumably due to him having a good night's sleep and the calm country air taking its effect. We rolled into the supermarket car park and wandered over to the entrance. Mike picked up a basket and I did my best to fill it with items from the list.

We made a quick lap around the chilled foods section, finding everything we'd noted down, plus the replacement lasagne, then grabbed a bottle of sparkling water and headed for the tills. The shop wasn't that busy, but it seemed like everyone had finished and was looking for a checkout at the same time. I pointed to the two self-service tills over towards the door and ushered Mike in that direction.

We'd barely spoken to each other since getting into the car, but the silence was soon shattered by my having to bark instructions at Mike, who had never used the self-serve tills before.

I scanned the items while Mike bagged, except he couldn't let go of anything once he'd bagged it and constantly tried to rearrange things, much to the automated voice's disgust.

'Please put the item back in the bagging area.' it said firmly, and slightly patronisingly.

Each time I just looked disappointedly at him to reinforce the message. I carried on scanning and passing items to Mike who, by now, was frantically dropping them onto the bagging area and dramatically moving his hands upwards as though surrounded by armed police. The automatic voice stopped nagging, as did I. Until I'd pressed the 'finish shopping and pay' button, at which point Mike looked at me blankly as if I was going to pay.

'Credit card!' I barked loudly, startling him slightly and causing him to forget which pocket his wallet was in. At that point I had noticed that a few customers and staff were looking around, so I decided to tone my voice down slightly, I didn't want to emasculate him as most other women in supermarkets try to do with their male companions.

I made a joke about technology to lighten the mood, Mike forced an uneasy smile, mainly in the direction of the other customers who still stared on.

The number of people looking at us seemed to have increased dramatically. One man stood with a newspaper in hand, looking directly at me, then Mike, then back at his newspaper, then back to me again. We both began to feel a little conspicuous and hurried out of the shop with our haphazardly packed carrier bags. We tossed them into the boot of the car and headed back to Ivy Cottage. As we embarked upon the short journey back I felt bad for being a bit of a brat, I blamed the tiredness and Mike nodded as if to accept my excuse and the implied apology.

We pulled back up to the cottage and Mike – managing to do a much better job of finding the entrance – gently eased into the gravel driveway, this time avoiding spraying stone chips into the neighbouring trees. I hopped out and opened the boot to grab the shopping before Mike had the chance to finish making whatever checks it is men make before getting out of a car. He got out just as I was slamming the boot and so walked straight to the front door to open it, while I headed through to the kitchen to put the shopping down.

It was mid-morning by this time, I was flagging slightly having been up so early, so I flopped on the sofa in the living room face down for a few minutes, hoping to be undisturbed. It probably didn't look the most comfortable position imaginable as Mike walked in and lightly snorted with laughter. He mentioned that we'd stupidly replaced the lasagne we ate yesterday but hadn't bought anything for that night's dinner. I snorted with laughter back at him and stayed prostrate on the sofa. Mike left me alone to finish putting away the shopping and look for a cool bag to take with us on our picnic.

I hadn't drifted off to sleep, just rested my eyes. As such I was conscious enough to realise that I would inevitably get sofa lines on my face should I lay in this position any longer, so I stood up, far too quickly, and flopped down on the sofa again. The second attempt was much more successful, in that I was able to stand for longer than half a second. I wandered out to the kitchen to find Mike, to ascertain what time we were heading out and in what direction.

'So where exactly are we going for this walk and picnic?' I asked tentatively.

'Well I've been for a few walks with Pete and Carol before, most of the area around the village is good for walking.' said Mike. 'There's a nice sort of pond and also a copse somewhere, but I must confess I'm not sure exactly how we got there. I'm sure we can just set off and see where the wind takes us. We can stop for our picnic wherever you want.'

'Ok, that sounds good to me, I like exploring.' I replied, excited at the thrill of the unknown.

In my mind, I had already played out the romantic walk a couple of times, although the visions were inconsistent. The unfamiliar nature of the upcoming journey reconciled with my feelings about Mike and my relationship. Setting off into the unknown might lead me to the place I wished for, taking Mike further out of his comfort zone and allowing me to take more control of our time together. Most of all I wanted our walk to feel new, as if charting a course down an untrodden path, so that I could make fresh, bright memories to replace the dark ones that consumed my idle moments.

In the absence of anything more suitable, I lent Mike my backpack, into which he packed the sausage rolls, scotch eggs, pork pies and quiche, as well as his camera and my magazine. He slipped the bottle of drink in a side compartment and put it by the door. He turned to me and appeared to look me up and down.

'Is that what you're wearing?' he said, before adding 'That's probably a good idea to wear something comfortable as we might be walking through overgrown paths and all sorts.'

'Oh no,' I replied, 'I'll be roasting in this if it gets much warmer out, I'd be more comfortable in something a little less restrictive.'

I didn't wait for a response or an argument on the matter. I darted straight into my bedroom to get changed into my new dress that I'd left hanging on the door. I pushed the door behind me, the hanger over the top stopped it from closing all the way and it swung back open slowly as I was getting changed.

I didn't feel like I had anything to worry about in that respect anymore, so I left it half open and continued undressing. I put on my second best bra and knickers, one of the sets I'd persuaded my mum to buy me, then eased my new dress over my head before tugging it down over my hips where it had gathered.

I scanned the room for a mirror. One hadn't magically appeared since last night so I peeked through into the hallway to make sure Mike wasn't around. I picked up a small carrier bag and ran to the bathroom to apply the finishing touches to my outfit. I didn't want to wear make-up, it was too heavy and I'd be in it all day while walking around the countryside sweating.

Instead I straightened my dress further, opened up the little carrier bag and pulled out the lip gloss I'd bought in London. I pouted into the bathroom mirror and applied a liberal coating to my lips, turning them from a soft neutral tone to a light pink, that matched one of the colours on my dress.

I returned the lip gloss to my wash bag and took one last look in the mirror. I wasn't sure who it was, but the girl staring back at me definitely reminded me of someone. I shook the thought from my head and turned round and exited the bathroom. I could hear Mike putting his shoes on in the living room and so I slipped on mine and stood in the doorway with my hands behind my back.

'Ready?' I asked with a smile.

'Yeah I'm just...' he started, before turning his head to make eye contact. 'well don't you look summery?'

'Thanks, I'm glad you like it. You look nice too in that brightly coloured polo shirt.' I said, seizing my opportunity to take care of step three of the magazine article's five step plan.

'Very kind of you to say so.' said Mike, instead sensing I was simply being polite.

'Anyway I wanted to wear this dress for you today.' I said, moving on.

'For me?' replied Mike, clearly confused by the statement.

'Well I wanted you to see me wearing it, you *did* buy it for me, and who knows when you might get to see it again?'

My question was rhetorical but he chose to answer it anyway.

'Why wouldn't I get to see it again?' he asked.

'Well it's nearing the end of summer and I'll be back in boring grey suburbia soon.' I replied.

'Oh right yes, of course you will.' said Mike in a very matter of fact way. 'Come on then, let's go.'

He brushed past me in the doorway on his way to the hall. This time there was nothing sensual about our fleeting contact, he practically pushed me into the door frame. It seemed strange, I couldn't work out whether something was wrong or perhaps I'd upset him, so I just turned and followed him towards the front door where he stood waiting for me, looking somewhat glum.

'Is everything ok?' I asked, determined to know if I was at fault.

'Yeah, yeah, sorry, just something on my mind, forget about it.' he replied, this time forcing a wide smile and putting me somewhat at ease.

Mike picked up the backpack, leaving me nothing to carry and making me feel strangely aware of my hands. I clasped them back behind me and skipped through the door Mike had just opened. We walked to the end of the driveway and Mike signalled to go right.

'What's right?' I asked.

'It's just the way we usually walk, I've never been left out of here.' said Mike.

'Left it is then.' I said cheerily, before grabbing Mike's hand and leading him off into the unknown.

Chapter 20

I had initially only grabbed Mike's hand in order to steer him in the direction I had wanted. A few hundred yards down the country lane, I realised I was still holding it. My grip had loosened somewhat but he hadn't pulled away. I certainly wasn't about to, part four or the magazine's five point plan was adamant that this contact was important. We remained hand in hand on our romantic walk, out of the other side of the village to which we'd always entered thus far. I periodically peered over at Mike who seemed perfectly comfortable walking with me this way. It was only when we got to a stile that he relinquished my hand as I clambered over.

There were little coloured arrows on the stile, presumably signifying walking routes, though we had no maps or guides to interpret them. Once Mike had clambered over with the backpack we stopped for a few seconds, to get our bearings and identify landmarks so we'd avoid getting lost. We decided to head straight across the field, hoping to pick up another stile or gate with more coloured arrows. This time I made no excuses as I offered my hand to Mike. He reached out and took it again, perhaps thoughtfully and deliberately, perhaps instinctively, I wasn't able to tell – but then I wasn't that concerned.

As we strolled through the field I glanced up at the pale sky and then back down to the lush green surroundings at eye level. As I looked closely at the grass beside the path it was a dark and a somewhat dull green, with hints of brown at the tips. Looking across the entire field, however, it was bright and vibrant, especially against the backdrop of the darker green trees that surrounded it. The sheer abundance of verdant shades caused everything to take on a greenish hue, the light reflected off the grass and onto my legs and tricked the eye into thinking me some alien visitor to this world.

The air was quite still, but the occasional breeze caught my dress and shifted it either left, against my empty hand, or right, playfully grazing the back of Mike's. The dress wasn't loose enough to be blown too violently and risk wardrobe malfunction, so I was enjoying giving it the freedom to go where it wanted.

I controlled the pace at which we walked, since we were connected, slowing it fractionally as we got halfway across the field. Here, at the furthest possible distance between stiles – with an eye-line all the way across the field – I felt happiest in our isolation. This was a place for Mike and me and no-one else. I wanted this mid-point to last forever, but seconds later I sensed the next stile approaching and the increased risk of bumping into well-meaning, but talkative ramblers.

We reached the other side of the field, with some more coloured way-markers pointing in various directions. We opted to follow the green arrow diagonally across the next field and while we did so we talked about nature and the great outdoors. We discussed soft grass under bare feet, the smell of wild flowers growing in the hedgerows, the crisp leaves that littered the floor of densely wooded areas. As we did so our pace slowed again. On occasion we turned inwards to face each other and used our free hands to describe shapes or point to objects with.

I thought that I would be sated by holding Mike's hand in this way. That doing so would calm my nerves and go some way towards satisfying my urges. Instead, it just unlocked new urges. Satisfaction remained painfully out of reach.

I held his hand and occasionally ran the tips of my fingers over his knuckles, as if by accident. I now wanted to run my fingers elsewhere, up his forearm, across his shoulder, up the side of his neck and behind his head. More importantly I yearned more than ever for his touch. I wanted to use the grip I had on his hand to guide it closer to me.

In the action of walking, with our arms swinging, I was once or twice able to graze my hip with the back of his hand. Each time we touched I breathed in deeply through my nose, my eyes closing involuntarily.

I felt overcome by these new feelings and so, spotting another green way-marker up ahead, I was keen to sit down for a rest. As we walked the last stretch, it was as though I could feel every inch of my body, the light breeze only heightening the sensation. I was also uncomfortably aware of my underwear pressing against my sensitive skin. I needed the opportunity to stop all movement, to remain perfectly still in order to allow this fierce intensity to subside.

I spotted a tree stump up ahead, one that looked like it had been smoothed over time by fellow weary travellers in need of a place to sit. I let go of Mike's hand, more permanently this time, and made my way over to the stump and sat with my legs stretched out in front of me. Mike sat next to me, though thankfully not too close, and opened the bottle of drink from the side of my backpack.

'Thirsty?' he said, offering me the first sip.

I tried to speak but my mouth felt like it was full of cotton wool. So instead I smiled, reached out my hand to grab the drink, and gulped down a third of the bottle in a distinctly unladylike fashion.

'I'll take that as a yes!' said Mike with a chuckle.

'Sorry, yeah. I didn't realise how thirsty I was until you asked.' I said, handing back the bottle.

I lowered my head and looked in the direction of my legs, my toes pointed out in front. I straightened the hem of my dress over my knees and looked at my calves and ankles in more detail. I had a few red patches of skin, a small bruise and an insect or two crawling on one leg.

I wasn't wearing any socks, my ankles looked like they had been thrashed by the thick grass as I walked. I didn't care though, I felt that these minute blemishes complimented the wearing of a summer dress. To wear a flowing floral dress indoors, with manicured hands and feet and shiny waxed calves, was to miss the point of summer.

'Hungry yet?' asked Mike.

'Yes, but I don't want to eat here.' I said in reply. 'Let's go and find a nice quiet field and sit right in the middle of it.'

'Ok, let me know when you're ready to set off again.' he said.

I nodded and shifted my gaze from my legs to the surrounding view. We were sat on the corner of a wooded area, possibly a copse, I had no real expertise to draw on in determining that. The shade helped cool my legs and the sensitive areas in between. My arms, however, were beginning to feel slightly chilly, so I was keen to at least get that part of me back into direct sunlight. My hair was a mess, I'd reached back to sweep it onto one shoulder and it didn't seem to want to be directed. I would have to deal with it when we sat down for our picnic.

I pressed my hands into the tree stump to help myself up, then stood and dusted myself down, rubbing my palms together to shift the dirt I'd picked up. One thing I did dislike about the great outdoors, was the lack of hand sanitation.

Mike remained seated, staring off into the distance, clearly daydreaming. I pondered the best way of rousing him, but most of my thoughts were rather more *arousing* than rousing. I instead opted just to walk right in front of him and stand there silently. He tilted his head back and refocused his eyes on me, before standing up in the little bit of room I'd left him between the tree stump and myself.

I picked up my backpack from the floor and put it over one shoulder. It was heavier than I had thought it would be, so I forced my other arm through the opposite strap and wore it on both. Its weight meant it sat very low against the small of my back and the straps dug into the edges of my chest. It had the side-effect of altering the neck line of my dress, making my breasts stick out and seem fuller than they actually were. The sore shoulders were a price I was willing to pay for this unintended boon and I stared at my chest for a good few seconds in amazement. I offered my left hand to Mike this time, he once again obliged and held it as we set off.

Around the corner from the shaded area was another wooden post with markings on, this time only green and red arrows were left. Red pointed towards a field with a barn and a couple of corrugated iron farm buildings, green pointed up the side of the copse towards a slightly sloped green field, a little more out of the way. Naturally, I followed the green symbol and before long we were halfway up the incline. I stopped and tugged at Mike's hand, insisting we head straight into the middle of the field.

Chapter 21

Mike turned to face back down the embankment and surveyed the vista before us. From here we could see for miles. The copse, the farm buildings, the main road into the village and the village itself in the distance.

'It certainly is quite a view Rebecca, I'll give you that. Ok come on then.' He said, striding into the centre with a care free gait.

I on the other hand, walked a little more carefully, so as to not lose my footing and fall, no doubt squashing the picnic food I carried on my back. I made my way over to Mike who stood proudly, dead centre in the middle of the field. We both looked at each other, half-expecting someone to pull out a picnic blanket. Alas we had none – neither of us had thought of that. Instead I took the backpack off my shoulder and placed it down in front of us, where it promptly fell forward with a dull thud. We sat down on the grass and opened it up to check the contents.

'What do you want first?' asked Mike, rummaging around in a melee of clear plastic containers.

'I don't mind, whatever you find first.' I replied.

He handed me a packet of two scotch eggs, then pulled out a pair of pork pies and sat the packet on his lap. At this time, the sun had just hidden behind a cloud, throwing a gradual darkness over our once delightful view, the colours muted and the temperature felt like it dropped in tandem. We tucked into our smorgasbord of picnic treats, carefully holding down plastic containers so that they didn't fly away in the light breeze. We'd worked up quite an appetite with our walk, so I wasn't in the least bit concerned about scoffing copious amounts of pastry goods, even sneaking one or two extra cocktail sausages while Mike wasn't looking. A short, sporadic conversation broke out between bites.

'So what's your favourite colour?' I childishly asked.

Mike shifted his legs slightly to face me before answering.

'Blue, I suppose.'

'You suppose?' I replied, 'what sort of blue, baby blue, royal blue, navy blue, midnight blue?'

I took another handful of cocktail sausages from the open packet and popped one from my hand to my mouth.

'Sort of normal blue I guess, like my car.' said Mike. 'Is that royal blue?'

'Yeah I think so.' I responded, considering whether I'd packed my blue underwear set.

'How about you, what's your favourite colour?' asked Mike.

'Oh that's easy,' I replied, 'purple all the way.'

'Ah, the colour of royalty. Fitting for a Princess I suppose.' said Mike with a cheeky wink.

'Is it? What makes it the colour of royalty?' I asked, 'I never see any princesses dressed in purple.'

'No that's true, but it used to be. I think the dye that they used to make clothes purple was once very expensive. Only the very wealthy, like the nobility, could afford it.'

'Well aren't you full of useless knowledge?' I said, picking up the last cocktail sausage from the pack. 'Last one!' I said, sitting up on my knees and holding it out just in front of Mike's face.

This time, unlike before with the travel sweet, he leant forward and aggressively snatched it out of my hand with his teeth, with an accompanying snarling sound. I pulled my fingers away sharply in shock, before laughing uncontrollably as he smiled at me with the sausage still protruding from his mouth.

When he allowed himself to cut loose and be silly, he was like a totally different person. He was relaxed, jovial, bordering on playful. It was an attractive quality which, although it reminded me of how he played with me when I was a child, didn't make me feel childish, but instead made him appear younger.

When we'd packed away all the food in our stomachs and all the wrappers in the backpack, we sat up and breathed a sigh of contentment and relief. Our fullness meant we wouldn't be moving any time soon.

As luck would have it, the large cloud had mostly passed across the sun and the edges of it turned golden as a sign of the impending brightness. We sat and watched, waiting patiently for the glimmering edges and fleeting pulses of light to become a full on burst of direct sunlight and warmth. When it finally came the light instantly caught our faces and caused a prickly sensation on my cheeks.

In an act of complete surrender, I lay back on the grass, my face still bathed in the sun due to the incline of the hill. I stretched my toes out, kicked off my pumps and spread my legs slightly further than would ordinarily be considered decent. The mixture of sunlight and occasional breeze was intoxicating, the sun warmed the areas that needed warming and the breeze cooled any areas that were uncomfortably hot. Mike offered me my magazine to read, but I was happy just as I was.

Mike remained upright, with his arms outstretched behind him, pinned into the slope like a couple of tent pegs. His knees were bent so the soles of his shoes were planted to the grass of the hillside. In this semi-reclined position his chest stuck out, affording me a glimpse of his pectoral muscles and the merest hint of the shape of a nipple through his thick polo shirt.

It was a sight that came at a cost, since the sun drove its light fiercely into my eyes each time I dared to look. But look I did, two or three times, before squeezing my eyelids more tightly as they began to water. My hands remained by my side, palms facing upwards. I felt around for Mike's hand but only the straps of the backpack between us were available to my grasp, so I gave up and drifted into a daydream.

As I lay on the soft, warm grass, I became aware of my skin getting flushed. The sort of dry, itchy heat, that serves as a warning for the sunburn to come. I rolled over onto my front and folded my arms under my head to form a pillow. My head was turned away from Mike but somehow I got the distinct impression he was now looking at me.

'What?' I asked in a muffled voice, without lifting my head from my hands.

'Hmmm? Oh nothing.' replied Mike, 'I was just making sure you weren't getting burnt. I didn't know how long you were planning on laying there?'

'Just a bit longer.' I mumbled.

All went quiet again. Mike didn't allow himself to fully recline on the grass, preferring to stick to his semi-recumbent position. I still sensed his eyes occasionally on me, but I wasn't likely to complain. When I'd turned over onto my front I hadn't bothered to readjust my dress. In my somewhat tired and exhausted state I wasn't really able to determine where exactly it sat on my legs, but the prickly heat certainly felt like it crept all the way up to the backs of my knees this time.

The pale skin on my calves was beginning to burn much more quickly than my shins had, so after a few more minutes, I turned back over and sat up level with Mike. I crossed my arms on my knees and turned to look at him staring off into the distance.

I felt as comfortable as I ever had around him. I was really beginning to believe he could love me as I loved him. He'd held my hand ever so graciously on our romantic walk, maybe it was a concession to my enthusiasm, or perhaps he felt this connection too.

Since I'd laid down, my hair was even more tangled than it was before. It was also a little coarse and dried out from the sun, bordering on frizzy in fact. I couldn't really get a good look at it, but I was sure it would be horrific and I didn't want to walk back through the village looking a mess.

I began to attempt to comb it with my fingertips, fanning out my fingers and pulling them through the hair, all of which I'd moved to one side of my head. Mike turned from his view of the fields and appeared to watch as I did so. I liked when he looked at me, in whatever fashion and for however long, it filled me with a sense of self-importance and boosted my confidence no end.

I pulled my fingers through my hair a few more times and then dramatically swung all my hair over to the other side so it rested on my right shoulder this time. I turned my head slightly so as to make it easier to let my hair fall completely straight while I ran my fingers through it. I now faced Mike and smiled at him as I did so. He smiled back and seconds later, coyly turned away. Disappointed at the fact he felt he had to look away, I decided to take a chance on some more physical contact.

'Little help?' I said, hopefully.

'Hmm? You need help?' asked Mike, awkwardly.

'Well if you're just gonna sit there and watch me struggle,' I said, 'you might as well lend a hand.'

'Right, I guess that's fair.' he said. 'What do you need me to do?'

I patted the ground behind me, to signify that he had to shuffle over and sit there in order to help. He dutifully stood up, stepped across and sat behind me with his legs crossed. I remained facing forward, slightly nervous for the first time in a while, acutely aware that he was now very close to me, yet completely out of my eye-line. The sense of anticipation was making my heart flutter wildly in my chest.

'What am I supposed to do?' he asked.

'Just help me get some of the tangles out, make it a bit straighter for the walk back.' I replied.

He pushed his fingers into the wave of tangled blonde hair that presented itself, pulling them downwards incredibly gently, not even reaching the ends before removing them.

'Like that?' he asked.

'You can be a bit more forceful than that, you'll never get the tangles out otherwise.' I replied.

Somewhat reluctantly he put his fingers back in, just below my scalp and dragged them through my hair much more firmly the second time around.

Tugging at the more knotted areas, he caused my head to tilt back slightly, so I tensed my neck muscles to keep it steady. He ran his fingers down a couple more times, each time pulling at the roots of the follicles in my scalp and causing tiny painful sensations that were oh so pleasurable in their own unique way. I wished like mad for his hands to wander elsewhere on my body. I felt sure that the merest touch of my bare shoulder right now would send me into convulsions.

'There, I think that's a bit better now.' he declared before standing back up and dusting off his jeans.

The period of physical contact was a little short-lived for my liking, but at least he'd been comfortable enough handling me in this way. I wished for him to kiss my bare neck or wrap his arms around my waist as he sat behind me, but all I could do was plant those seeds of thought in his mind. It would be up to him to act upon them. I couldn't possibly risk pushing things any further and end up losing him altogether.

In another burst of confidence, I leapt up, thanked him for helping, and planted a big kiss on his cheek, before turning and skipping off to the edge of the field to head back down. I daren't look back to see his reaction, or risk a telling off, but judging by the time it took for him to reach me at the side of the field, I had at least given him something else to think about.

When he appeared next to me, the now largely empty backpack draped loosely over his shoulder, he reached out, unprompted, and held my hand as we walked carefully back down the hill. Step four complete, I thought, as we headed through the fields, down the edge of the copse, over the various stiles and through the green-arrowed checkpoints.

My ankles and calves were beginning to hurt, I would be glad to get the weight off my feet when we got back. I suspected a foot massage would be out of the question, but I indulged myself with the thought of it nonetheless.

Chapter 22

We made it to back to Ivy Cottage's familiar gravel driveway, seemingly quicker than the walk to the hill, which was a relief. From our vantage point, on the outskirts of the village, we could see a group of people in the centre who seemed deep in conversation. It would be fair to say the level of conversation on *our* entire romantic walk and picnic was minimal. There was no particular reason for this, but having talked so much the previous night I was glad of the chance to let some things remain unsaid.

There was much to be said for comfortable silence. I had friends who feel the need to fill every void with idle chatter. Sometimes in awkward social situations it's a necessary evil, but the rest of the time it's just plain tiring.

As we entered the dark, cool, stone building, a strange feeling came over me. Neither Mike or I had explicitly stated, but I assumed that we would be heading back home tomorrow. I'd given vague instructions to my father of when to expect me back and although I hadn't exactly kept to my plans thus far, I suspected Mike would ensure I kept my word in terms of returning eventually.

The mere thought of ending this trip – coupled with being in that house with my father again – was simply too much to bear. I forced the thought from my mind and convinced my sub-conscious to subdue it until such a time as I could no longer afford to. I was surprisingly good at doing that, it was a technique that I developed naturally during and after my mum's illness.

Mike handed me my backpack – having cleared the plastic food wrappers from it – and I took it back into my bedroom. I pulled out my magazine and found Mike's camera underneath. I stared at it for a second before deciding to play a bit of a joke on him.

I lifted my dress over my head and threw it onto the bed, stood in just my underwear, then turned the camera on and snapped a cheeky picture that I hoped would make him smile when he next reviewed the photos. I quickly returned the camera to its case and put my dress back on so he'd be none the wiser. I left the bedroom with my magazine and the camera – which I left by the front door – before heading back into the living room.

For the first time on our trip I had allowed Mike to put the kettle on for our ritualistic cup of tea. I sat on the sofa with my feet up on a side table I'd positioned in front of me. I pulled off my socks to air my feet and left them by the fireplace. I could see a feint line on my ankles, a change of colour, which signified that I had caught the sun ever so slightly. I still looked relatively pale all over, but my feet now seemed white by comparison.

'We're out of milk.' shouted Mike from the kitchen.

I wasn't sure what I was supposed to do with the information. I didn't feel like getting back up again.

'Ok.' I shouted back as a vague response.

'I'll stick a note on the fridge to remind me to get some in the morning.' he continued.

He then proceeded to walk into the living room with two, darker than usual, cups of tea. He sat one down on the table in front of me, adjacent to my feet, uttering a cautionary 'be careful' as he did so. I leant forward to inspect the colour further, and picked it up gently before removing my feet from the table.

I'd had visions of my somewhat sweaty feet picking up the whole table, cup of tea and all. I needn't have worried, either about picking up the table, or the strength of the tea, which was most satisfactory. I took a quick sip, set it back down again and leant back into my chair to carry on reading.

'Tired?' asked Mike.

I nodded and reminded him I'd woken up early in my cold bedroom. I didn't feel it necessary to remind him of being woken up again in the bath.

'You'll sleep much better tonight in the main bedroom.' he said, surveying the sofa he was to make his bed later on.

As grateful as I was for letting me have his bed that night, I couldn't help feeling a little bad for him having to sleep on the sofa. It was no more than five feet wide, and somewhat tattered and tired in comparison to the armchairs that flanked it. At least he'd have the fire to keep warm, it would probably be the warmest room in the house overnight.

Mike picked up his book and I seized the opportunity to flick from an agony aunt page back to my 'Five steps to snag your man' article for the last time.

"Step five: Leave on a high.

As tempting as it is to stay in his presence, you need to find a suitable time to part company and leave him wanting more. Don't talk until you've run out of things to say, set a time that you need to leave by, even if it means cutting off an interesting conversation mid-flow. Hopefully he'll be disappointed that your time together is up and will be more likely to want to see you again."

I wasn't really sure what to make of step five. After all, I didn't really have anywhere to go. We were pretty much stuck together and up to this point that had worked quite well for me. I decided to ignore that piece of advice for now and discarded the magazine on the floor next to me.

I drank my tea, which, due to its strength, seemed to send caffeine coursing through me more quickly than usual and perked me up. It wasn't long before I was wide awake, sufficiently rested and getting bored again. I fidgeted a few times, my eyes darted around the room, from the view of the garden, to the empty fireplace, with the occasional stolen glance at Mike in between. Finally I plucked up the courage to speak.

'Let's play a game then.' I said, aware that we'd missed out on that particular form on entertainment the night before.

'Yeah ok, shall we go into the dining room to play?' replied Mike.

'Nah, let's set one up on one of the tables in here, we can push the chairs closer together if necessary.' I suggested, still not wanting to move my body despite my mind's new-found energy.

'I'll bring in a couple from which to choose then.' said Mike, hopping up from his chair.

He returned seconds later with three brightly coloured boxes.

'Ok, one of these you have to draw what's on the card. Another you have to make it out of plasticine. The last one is just trivia questions, it's the 21st Century edition so you might know some of the answers.'

'The trivia one sounds good.' I replied, realising that it would also involve the least movement.

Mike set up the game board and playing pieces on the table between us. I then casually pushed it closer to him with my foot, so he'd be in control of it. He handed me a little box of questions to ask him when it was his turn. I suspected I'd be asking more questions than I would be answering. I selected the pink playing piece and rolled the dice from my laid back position, nearly causing it to fall off the small table.

The questioning began. As it turned out, I knew an awful lot more than I would have expected. The questions seemed to be exclusively about current affairs, music, films and TV programmes from the last ten years or so. I had passively absorbed enough knowledge from sitting in the same room as the news when my mum had watched it, plus there was nothing I didn't know about music and films from my magazines. Any in-depth political or historical questions were lost on me, but as Mike gobbled up those questions I played tactically and avoided relying on them.

On the odd occasion I did answer one of the more highbrow questions correctly, the look on Mike's face was priceless. A mixture of confusion and admiration, with what I liked to think was a *soupçon* of lust or longing. I played it cool and reacted with a calm sense of expectancy, even though I was stunned at my own quizzing prowess. I took my cues on this from Mike, who had a vast range of knowledge, answering questions on subjects I struggled even to pronounce. Each time he did I grew more impressed, if it was possible to be more impressed by someone I already had total and utter adoration for.

The game lasted for an hour or so, by the end I was leant forward on my chair excitedly barking out answers in an attempt to thwart my foe and establish my dominance over him. To do so would help with my plan, to take him out of his comfort zone and hopefully glimpse behind the facade I suspected he often put up around me. As we both neared the middle of the board I wasn't about to let up, answering questions correctly on dance music, horror films and UK Prime Ministers to wrap up a closely fought victory. I leapt up into the air and celebrated with a little jig, much to Mike's amusement. I think I cared more about the result than he did, but I still lorded it over him for the remainder of the afternoon.

I volunteered to put the game away while Mike wandered out into the kitchen to look for what to cook for dinner that night. As I picked up the loose question cards on Mike's side of the table I couldn't help noticing he'd added a few additional clues into some of the questions he'd just asked me that had closed out the match in my favour. I convinced myself that I'd have got them anyway, and so my victory was, to my mind, a fair and just one.

I put the games away in the dining room and went to see if Mike needed any help in the kitchen. When I arrived he was again hidden in a cupboard, this time a different one from the one that kept the cereals. I stayed silent in the doorway, I'd seen enough slapstick comedy to know that if I spoke or crept up behind him he'd hit his head on the top of the cupboard. I then considered whether him sustaining concussion might help my cause somewhat, but the thought of that distracted me from the fact he had finished and was stood up already.

'Pasta again?' said Mike.

'Yeah, don't worry, I love pasta, have we got any sauce though?' I asked.

'Well there's a jar of red pesto in the fridge and plenty of olive oil if that's ok?' he replied.

'Sounds good to me. Shall I lay the table?'

'Yeah if you want, that would be helpful.' he said.

I set about gathering the cutlery, placemats, some glasses and the candle from on top of the cupboard in the dining room. I wondered whether some alcohol might help bring down Mike's defences a little more. He was certainly far more talkative that night in his hotel room. I went to look around the kitchen discreetly while he sourced pots and pans with which to cook. I was rather conspicuous in my search and had soon bumped into him as I made my way around.

'What are you looking for Becky?' he asked.

'Oh, I was just looking to see if they had any wine we could open.'

'I think the wine rack is in the cupboard under the stairs, do you know what you're looking for?'

Of course I didn't know what I was looking for, but I had noticed that most bottles of wine had printed on the back which foods they made ideal accompaniments for.

'Something that goes with pasta and tomato dishes.' I shouted as I made my way out of the kitchen towards the stairs.

I opened the cupboard and saw the huge wine rack with thirty or so bottles lined up neatly. The ones at the bottom looked dusty and horrible, so I decided I didn't want any of those. The ones on the top seemed much newer and cleaner, so I checked the back of two or three of them before eventually settling for a bottle of Rioja which confirmed its suitability on the back. I headed back to the kitchen to show Mike how expertly I'd selected the wine for that night.

'I've got a 2011 'Rio-Jar' that says it goes well with rich tomato dishes." I exclaimed, with less than expert pronunciation.

'Hah, it's "Re-och-er" darling.' said Mike, grabbing it off me with a smile. 'Did they have more than one of these?'.

'Yeah there was a couple of them in there.' I replied, still shocked at what he'd just called me.

'Ok that's great, thanks for doing that.' he said, returning to his pots and pans.

I left the kitchen and sat back in my armchair in the living room, to ponder the thought of being his darling. It was amazing how one word could make you feel. A simple combination of letters, forming two curt syllables, caused a stir deep inside me. The fact that the word came at the end of a sentence designed to ridicule me was immaterial. I just sat and repeated the word over and over silently in my head for a few minutes. When Mike called out for some help in the kitchen it took all the strength I had not to shout back 'Okay, darling'.

When I entered the kitchen, Mike was wrestling with an extremely large pan of water – within which the pasta was swimming around – holding if aloft over the sink and motioning with his eyes and head to the sieve. I assumed I was supposed to hold it in case it slipped under the weight of water he was about to pour through it. I did as instructed by his body language and leant my head back away from the onslaught of steam as he poured. In his keenness not to spill any Mike leant his head over the sink and took the brunt of the scalding vapour which covered his face like a fine film of sweat.

After the commotion had died down, we returned the drained pasta to the bowl and stirred in most of the jar of pesto, before relenting and adding the remainder. The smell wafted up from the warm pasta and filled the room, causing me to salivate and reach a higher state of alertness. Mike grabbed some cheese he'd found in the fridge, and having decanted the coated pasta into large bowls, finely grated a smattering of it across the dish. There was a certain deliciousness in its simplicity, especially in comparison to the frozen lasagne that was far too uniform in shape and taste.

We each carried our own bowls into the dining room. Mike poured one large and one small glass of wine – for himself and me respectively – and we sat and tucked into our dinner. My mind wandered throughout, struggling to shift the thought of the previous night's conversation, one of bitterness and regret, sadness and ultimately futility.

I was determined not to repeat that gloomy affair and instead turned my mind to the question I'd been dying to ask for the last few days. I wanted to know who the woman was in the picture. I wanted to know why I'd never heard anything about her. I couldn't let on that I'd seen the photo in his bedroom drawer, but I had an ace up my sleeve, a single piece of information that – if my hunch proved correct – would blow the lid off this closely guarded secret.

Just as Mike brought a forkful of pasta towards his mouth I hit him with it.

'So, tell me about Marie?'

Chapter 23

It felt like a few minutes had passed since I'd asked my question. Mike had paused, stunned by the mention of Marie, his fork three-quarters of the way between bowl and mouth, where it remained for what seemed like an eternity. Small twirls of pasta clung together tightly atop, with only the viscosity of the pesto to bind them. Eventually this balancing act could continue no longer and a single piece tumbled, causing the rest to loosen their grip on the fork and forcing Mike to return both fork and pasta to the bowl.

'How do you know about Marie?' asked Mike, seemingly shocked, but not angry.

I smiled knowingly, intending to throw him off guard further, but also convince him it was ok to talk about it. I said nothing for a few moments, then when I sensed he was keen for an actual answer to his question I eventually replied.

'A girl hears things.' I said cryptically.

'From your mum?' he asked. 'It must have been from your mum because I never really told anyone. What did she tell you? How much do you know?'

By this point I felt a little guilty that I'd led him to believe I actually knew anything. All I had to go on was a photograph of Mike with a woman I'd never seen before. That and the fact he insisted on calling his wife Marie when we concocted our cover story. It was the speed with which that name came to him, coupled with the lack of alternatives he considered, that convinced me that Marie was the name of the woman in the photograph. That was still all I knew, but I felt I deserved to know more.

'I don't know anything.' I said. 'It's just a name I heard mentioned once or twice, I figured there was more to it than you were letting on.'

'Oh ok,' he replied, 'then it's nothing, nothing important.' He drunk some of his wine and put the half empty glass back on the table.

'If it's important to you, then it's important to me.' I said. These were words which I'd heard used before in such a context.

'I told you what was on my mind these last few days. I feel like you already know everything about me, but there's parts of you that are kept hidden. If it's good to talk about these things and a problem shared is a problem halved, then you can't really avoid telling me about Marie.' I concluded.

Mike sat solemnly for a minute, more troubled than ever by his thoughts. I'd backed him into a corner somewhat, by pleading to his sense of fairness given the revelations I'd shared with him of late. Although I was still keeping one pretty significant revelation close to my chest of course.

Finally, he inhaled, in a deliberate and languid manner, before sighing audibly and beginning to tell his story.

'Marie was my fiancée,' said Mike, in a short, sharp statement that shocked me into silence.

'We were together for three years in total. We were very much in love. At least I think we were, even now at my age, I'm not sure I know what love is.

'She was the girl Pete and I bonded over at school that day. We bumped into each other again at the hospital years later, where she was working as a nurse. Your mum knew her as well, if only by name.

'When Marie and I first started seeing each other things weren't always easy. She was jealous of the relationship I had with your mum. We were always joking and laughing in work – just trying to pass the time really – but if Marie caught us she'd grill me about it later on.

'Of course, things didn't get any better when your mum became ill and I started spending more time round at your house. I knew I wanted to help out, both for you and your mum's sake, but every time I did I knew I was hurting Marie more, and endangering everything that we'd built.

'I worked hard at the relationship. I'm not saying Marie didn't, but I felt like I was putting in so much effort to constantly appease her. I made bold gestures and displays of affection, especially around the hospital, just to convince her that she was the only one I loved.

'Of course in some ways that wasn't really true, I cared a great deal about you and your mum too.

'Marie and I went away on holiday last summer, just a short trip to a cabin in the countryside. It was there that I had decided to ask her to marry me. I still don't know if it was the right thing to do, but I felt like it was a good idea at the time. I loved her, I did want to be in a relationship with her, but I probably forced myself to ask her to marry me as an outward sign of reassurance.

'We had a beautiful week, the weather was warm, the cabin was peaceful, we just enjoyed each other's company. We went for long countryside walks, browsed the local antiques market, sat in a pub beer-garden on Sunday and talked about old times, how we'd been at the same school but never really spoken, our first dates together. It wasn't a deliberate attempt on my part to look wistfully at how happy we were and could be again, but it certainly didn't hurt.

'On the final day of our holiday, I slipped the ring I'd bought into my jacket pocket as we headed out for an early evening stroll. We walked up to a ridge just a few hundred yards from the cabin, sat on a dry stone wall and looked out across the countryside in the fading light. Then I plucked up the required courage to first stand up, then kneel down beside her. Her face was wracked with confusion, she hadn't seen it coming, but seconds later the ring was on her finger and we were locked in a tight embrace, nearly falling over the wall in the process.

'A few days later, however, things seemed to have cooled. She hadn't told her parents or friends, I hadn't told anyone either but that wasn't unlike me. She continued to ask questions and get angry whenever I came to visit you. I began to lie and make up excuses for why I was late home from work, or why I had to go out on a Sunday morning when I was taking you to hockey practice.

'Marie and I spent Christmas together, visiting my parents and hers too, but still not officially announcing our engagement. By then she had taken to only wearing the ring in my presence, it came off at night and each time she left the house, where it stayed in a little dish by the door, alongside miscellaneous keys. There were moments of genuine happiness, telling glances across the room while in company – little things that convinced me we'd make it through.

'A few days after Christmas, everything changed again. I was with Marie when I got the phone call from the hospital and rushed out without saying a word. I didn't have time for a row, or even to make up an excuse, I just left. When I eventually left you at the hospital with your father I just walked around outside for half an hour, scared to go home and face Marie. If she said anything that irked me I felt sure that, having just lost a close friend, I'd lose my temper and say or do something I'd regret.

'I eventually made my way home, later that evening and told Marie everything. She remained remarkably calm, didn't shout, didn't ask lots of questions or antagonise me. In fact she was incredibly supportive and comforted me, which was an unexpected yet welcome relief. Looking back I guess she interpreted the news as some sort of closure. A silver lining – for her at least – against the backdrop of dark clouds that hung over me at that time.

'Weeks went by, after the funeral, where we didn't fight at all. We just coexisted, peacefully, no longer butting heads all the time. The trust returned too, if I was late home from work or I disappeared for a few hours, she barely said anything at all. No longer was I held to account for my every move, forced to break down my day into its constituent parts and explain any gaps in the timeline. We became, dare I say, comfortable in our relationship. It had moved onto a new level, one of acceptance and contentment rather than romance and impulsion. She even started to wear her engagement ring again, I noticed its absence from the dish by the front door now and then.

'Then one day, when I came home from work, things had changed again. Nothing immediately seemed unusual, no foreboding dark skies over the house as I approached. I walked in and saw the engagement ring in the dish, but all else was quiet and undisturbed. The lights were off in the front room and sitting in the corner fully enveloped by shadow was Marie, the only light came from a mobile phone, my mobile phone, which I'd inadvertently left at home that day.

'As I approached her gingerly, she turned the phone around and the light shone in my face, temporarily blinding me and causing my eyes to take a moment to focus and read what was on the screen.'

At that point Mike paused his monologue and his head rose from the point on the dining table he'd been staring at the whole time – he now looked directly into my eyes as he spoke.

'It was a text message from you Becky. From the phone I'd given you after the funeral. It was short, totally devoid of context, it just said "*Hey, can you call me?*" or something to that effect. It was the first time Marie had seen one of your messages. I wasn't making a conscious effort to hide them, it was just coincidence that it had taken this long. I wasn't sure what Marie was thinking, but I sensed she was about to tell me in great detail.

'She flew into a rage almost immediately once I'd confirmed that the message was from you. She had convinced herself, in the two hours between getting home and finding the phone and me walking through the door, that there was something untoward in the relationship I had with you. 'Do you love her? she asked. A question I didn't answer quickly enough, which only gave further credence to her accusations.

'Regardless of what I said to allay her fears, Marie felt betrayed. She felt I'd deliberately kept my contact with you from her. Maybe I had, subconsciously or otherwise, I still don't know after all this time. Marie and I talked well into the night and although things calmed down and the language and tone softened slightly, Marie made one thing very clear. Either I stopped seeing or talking to you, or my relationship with her would be over.'

By this point in the story I was beginning to cry. But my lungs seemed equally in shock and so there was no noise, no sharp breathing, just tear after tear forming in the corners of my eyes and dripping down my face and dampening the tablecloth below. There was no-one to catch them this time. Mike had re-affixed his gaze to the spot on the table, his eyes wide, recanting the story with unerring detail as if he'd lived these moments over and over again in the months that followed. Bravely, he continued unabated.

'I lay awake all night that night, wondering how on earth I could tell *you*, the innocent party in all this – a girl who'd just lost her mother – never to call or message me again. I framed the sentiment in my mind several times, trying to find the words that would make such a statement alright, but of course none would. It was then that I realised that if I couldn't find the words, perhaps there were no words, and if there were no words then it was because it's a situation that should never arise. Nobody should be forced to make that declaration, and so – quite simply – I wouldn't.

'The following morning I informed Marie of my decision. I wouldn't give in to the ultimatum and abandon someone who needed me, just because *she* thought it unusual that I would still want that person in my life. This time she didn't scream and shout, just quietly packed some things and left, leaving her ring in the dish by the door on the way out. That was the last time I saw or spoke to her. She picked up the remainder of her possessions later that week while I was at work. I vowed to myself never to tell you what happened – I didn't think you needed to know.'

Mike looked up from the table once again, sniffed loudly and wiped a tear from his eye in order to look at me. I was still unable to speak and just stared blankly at him as I processed the vast amounts of information he'd relayed. It wasn't my intention to create a prolonged period of silence, or make either of us feel more awkward, but it served the purpose of making Mike feel instant regret for having told me.

'I'm so sorry, Rebecca, I shouldn't have said anything.'

'No, no...' I finally responded, having at least partly digested this revelation. 'I'm glad you did.'

I reached across the table, grabbed his hands and held them tightly. I had little concern for what was appropriate in the context of our relationship at this time, I did what I needed to show him how I felt.

'Thank you.' I said. 'Thanks for telling me this, thanks for standing up for me, thanks for keeping the promise you made to me at the hospital, for everything you've ever done for me, thank you.

'And I'm sorry,' I continued, 'sorry for being the person that cost you your happiness.'

'Don't apologise, please,' he interjected, 'you've got nothing to be sorry for. It was all my own stupid fault, I should have been more honest with Marie and maybe things would have been different.'

I felt compelled to disagree.

'I'm not sure things would.' I said sharply. 'I didn't know Marie, but I know you. You're a kind and decent guy, you were only trying to do what you thought was best. You were my mum's best friend, there was nothing wrong with that relationship, but Marie still didn't like you spending time with us. She put you in an impossible position, one that caused you to lie about your whereabouts.

'Her jealousy and demands over your time were at best unreasonable, if not downright unfair. You had a life before you met Marie, you had a friendship that was important to you and it wasn't right for her to try and guilt you into giving that up.'

'If you'd had a child from a previous marriage or something would she have demanded you stop seeing them too?' I finished angrily.

Mike let out a nervous chuckle, but didn't offer an opinion on whether he thought she would have made such demands.

'I guess what I'm trying to say is... It wasn't your fault Mike.'

'I know,' he replied, 'but you always wonder if maybe you could have done things differently.'

'Yes, but you can't fixate on it.' I said. 'You've been through so much yourself. I may have lost my mum but you also lost a close friend. On top of that you took on the responsibility of *my* emotional wellbeing. Perhaps it's time you looked after your own?'

I tried to make eye contact with him but he awkwardly shifted his gaze.

'You've spent so long trying to please other people,' I continued, 'juggling my mum's illness, my grief and Marie's needs, but who was there to look after your needs?'

'I guess I thought I could handle it.' he said. 'I tried to be strong for you and your mum.'

'I know, and you were. I couldn't have asked for a better person to help me through that. I know my mum was so grateful too. But if we'd known that it was to the detriment of your life and your relationship with Marie, maybe we wouldn't have relied on you so much.'

I paused and sighed loudly as I prepared myself to ask the next important question.

'You still think about her a lot, right?'

'Marie?' he asked.

'Yes, Marie. You still think about her and what might have been? You still have fond memories?'

'I guess so, sometimes. More over these last few days.'

'How come over these last few days?' I asked.

'Well sometimes you remind me of her. I'm not sure if that's a good thing for you to hear, but it's true. Sometimes the way you smile, or swing your hair across onto one shoulder, little mannerisms. In those moments, I think of her, with a mixture of fondness and sadness, and then I wonder if she was right all along.'

I wasn't sure either if that was something I wanted to hear, but any sense of pride, along with my own ambitions, were swept aside by my need to be there for Mike at this point. So I marginalised my own personal feelings about Marie and focused on helping Mike deal with the fact she was no longer a part of his life.

'They say time heals all wounds.' I offered, somewhat desperately.

'I hope so.' he said, with less confidence than me.

'I take it this is also why you were keen to take voluntary redundancy from your job?' I asked.

'Yeah. I decided I needed a clean break, a fresh start. I wasn't doing much with my new-found freedom though and that's why in some ways I was glad to hear from you the other night. The timing couldn't have been better really, it seemed like we both needed a break from our everyday lives.'

'Glad I could be of service.' I said with a cheeky grin.

Mike smiled, a wide, unforced, reactionary smile.

'Hug?' I suggested, again for mutually beneficial, yet wholly unromantic reasons.

'Sure.' he replied.

He stood up, with one arm outstretched across the table – retaining a constant physical connection between us – as he made his way to the side of the table and pulled me in close to him.

This embrace was unlike any other we'd had before, it felt more reciprocal, less fatherly, dare I say less patronising. Mike was also far more relaxed, he didn't seem nervous, awkward, or keen to break the embrace as soon as he could. Instead we just held each other, my arms tucked under his and folded across the his back, my hands against his shoulder blades, his arms lower, around my waist, with his hands reaching right the way across my back to the opposite sides.

My head was pressed against his chest but in a change to previous embraces it was turned to face him instead of looking away. From here he rested his chin against the top of my head gently. As he did so he allowed his right hand to rub gently against my side, through my dress, just above the hip, shifting the material up and down by an inch or so as he did. In response I stroked the area above his right shoulder blade with my thumb. We continued in this exact pattern for a minute or so, allowing the soothing motions of each other's hands to massage some of the stresses from our bodies and minds.

I tilted my head slightly to look up at Mike, hoping to catch his eye. Alas, he was so close to me, it was almost impossible for my eyes to focus. As I attempted to do so, he kissed me softly and protractedly on the forehead. I gripped his shoulder blades even more tightly in an autonomous fashion at being kissed like this, before tilting my head back down and pressing it further into his chest.

'Better?' he asked.

'Almost.' I replied, wanting to use up my full quota of affection before letting him go.

I gave one final squeeze before releasing my grip and stepping back one pace. As I did so he ran his hands along the outside of my upper arms and down my forearms, until once again he held me by the fingertips. We looked at each other and smiled in silent reverence. He may not have wanted to admit it, but I knew our relationship had changed now, for the better as far as I was concerned.

'You know what?' he said. "You surprise me sometimes."

'How so?' I asked.

'You're very perceptive. Sometimes you can read what I'm feeling so accurately. You definitely have a way of cutting through all the nonsense too, seeing a situation for what it is. Stripping away all the politics, all the confused emotion that clouds our judgement, then delivering an insightful yet succinct verdict.'

It probably helped that I didn't have any experience of such politics or contradictory emotions in my relationships. At my age things were a lot more black and white. Perhaps he mistook my naivety for clarity, my directness for insight. Perhaps that wasn't a mistake at all to judge them as such. Maybe I could offer him a lucidity that someone older than me – more experienced in such situations – simply couldn't. I distilled this down into a response he'd be more comfortable hearing.

'I just speak as I find.'

'Yes, indeed you do.' he said, laughing somewhat under his breath and picking up his half full wine glass and taking a sip.

I picked up mine and proposed a toast.

'To doing what's best for us.' I said.

'To us.' Mike responded, clinking his glass into mine.

I finished my small glass of wine, which was much more pungent and flavourful than I was used to. My tongue felt like it had been coated with a layer of the fur you find on fresh blackberries. I shuddered slightly and poked out my tongue to try and aerate it.

Mike suggested I go and get some water so I left the room and filled up my wine glass from the kitchen tap before returning.

The candle on the table had now burnt down about halfway. The base was thicker than before with melted and cooled wax. The light it created flashed through the wine glasses it was now level with and refracted against the walls and in turn, our faces. It somehow made Mike look withered and old, presumably it made me look the same. I smiled to myself at the thought of recreating this scene without the candlelight and glasses someday.

Suddenly, and unexpectedly, I let out a huge yawn which I was powerless to stop. In fact I only just managed to raise my hand to my mouth in time to stop Mike getting an unsolicited view of my tonsils. I looked at the clock in the dining room, which signalled that it was just before 10pm. I remembered how I'd been up at around 6am and except for a brief period of rest for my eyes while in the bath, I had been awake for a long time now. My brain was sending me signals that were frankly unwelcome, I wanted to stay up talking and sharing things with Mike for as long as I could.

I soldiered on for another five minutes, engaging Mike in a conversation about his work and what he might do next. I couldn't stifle another yawn though and Mike chose to read that as a sign that I was bored of hearing about his career options. If I'm honest it wasn't the most thrilling conversation in the world, but I felt extremely grown up for starting it. I attempted to assure him I was ok to carry on talking, but as I yawned again half way through this defiant last stand I had proved the validity of his argument.

I made my way to the bathroom to clean my teeth and get ready for bed. As I stood in front of the mirror brushing, the minty flavour of the toothpaste temporarily jarred my senses and woke me up somewhat. I remembered that we hadn't lit that fire that we'd planned in order to keep the living room warm for Mike overnight. We'd talked for so long that I'd forgotten all about it, I assumed Mike had too. As I left the bathroom I saw him through the living room doorway, fixing the cushions on the sofa into the best arrangement for sleeping.

'We didn't light the fire.' I said, stating the obvious.

'Yeah, I know, I completely forgot, don't worry though, it'll be ok.' he replied unconvincingly.

'Don't be silly, you'll freeze to death in here.' I said dramatically. 'Just come and sleep in there with me, there's plenty of room.'

'No, honestly, I'll be fine.' he said.

'I don't take up that much room. What are you trying to say?' I said jokingly. He chuckled as he looked at me, which delayed his inevitable response.

'Look,' I said, cutting in before him, 'I'll go and get into bed. I'll sleep right over to one side and you'll see there's plenty of room for you. I'll be asleep in no time anyway, when I wake up I expect to find you there next to me.'

With that, I strode out of the living room and into the master bedroom, leaving the door ajar slightly as I closed it, to let him know I was serious. I was pleased with my exit from the room, one that I hoped was sufficient to cover step number five in the magazine's five step plan. I certainly felt like I'd left the room on a high.

I realised I was still wearing my summer dress. I hadn't brought my bed-shirt in with me but I couldn't very well go and get it now and ruin my dramatic exit. I pulled the dress over my head and got into bed with my underwear on before removing the bra and socks under the covers and placing them beside me on the floor.

I lay motionless, my arms beside me, the covers pulled tightly over my bare chest, my body right over to one side of the mattress as promised. As soon as I closed my eyes I sensed my brain disengage slightly, my eyelids felt heavy and everything faded to black.

Chapter 24

I became aware of footsteps, then a faint light leaking from the hallway told me that the door to the bedroom had been opened. The light penetrated my eyelids and was processed by my brain as a warm yellow glow. The footsteps, although light, grew louder, less distant. The sound reverberated around the room, but the source was unmistakeably alongside me now, level with my head. As the light from the hallway faded and the door swung to, a new light, hotter and whiter than the previous one, replaced it. The footsteps grew faint again and the light dimmed, the sound of running water in the distance told me the footsteps had now made their way into the en-suite bathroom.

I remained motionless on the bed, eyelids fixed tightly, as though gripped by fear and anticipation. With one sense dulled I was able to make out the distinct sounds of different flow rates of water, a tap, a toilet flushing, a cistern refilling. It was the last of these that signalled an end to the routine and caused the white light to return, albeit briefly, before the whole room was once again plunged into darkness. Now with no light or sound to process I had a heightened awareness of this mysterious individual carefully lifting up one corner of the duvet and sliding their body under it.

The bed I occupied had the faintest aroma of the previous night's incumbent. I'd been comforted by the smell before, it was familiar without being overly so. I hadn't got used to this smell the way one gets used to the smell of one's own clothes or bedroom. It assaulted my olfactory glands and became more pungent that I'd ever experienced before. The feint lingering of scent on fabric were now replaced by the raw, unfettered smell of the true living source. Unmistakeable proof that now, beside me in this bed, he lay. His name no longer prefixed or familiarised, just plain, yet oh so wonderful, Mike.

I cast my mind back over the series of events that had conspired to bring us together, here in this bed, at this precise moment. My mother's death and the subsequent arguments I had with my father; Mike's relationship with Marie ending; him leaving his job; and finally a broken storage heater. All of these things and many more, some life-changing and some trivial, had brought us to this point, brought me closer than I'd ever been to the man I believed I loved. It would have been a crime to let this moment pass and so I reached out my hand, as I had done earlier in the day, hoping to grasp at his.

My eyes remained closed and every part of my body that could keep still did so, the extension of my arm was almost autonomous, like a muscle spasm that would occur during a deep sleep. On this occasion, my outstretched hand was met with another, larger hand, with thicker fingers, wider knuckles and ever so slightly coarser flesh. The larger hand reciprocated by holding the smaller, more frail and soft-skinned hand tightly, squashing it into the mattress, almost uncomfortably.

I lay like this for a minute, the initial satisfaction of holding hands soon waning and creating urges for more. More contact, more of his skin against my skin, more of everything – just more. I arched up my thumb from beside my fingers and used it to gently stroke the soft skin of his wrist. Not soft in comparison to my wrist, but soft in comparison to his palm. After three slow back and forth motions, I could sense I wasn't the only one craving more contact.

He shifted onto his side violently in one motion, causing the mattress to list to one side and my body to edge slightly closer to the middle. I was no longer right over to one side of the bed as had been promised. His left hand remained enveloped in my right, but from his new position his right hand had been freed and carefully made its way across from his body towards mine. I could feel the duvet moving upwards slightly as the hand pressed up against it on its journey, creating a peak that ran from left to right until it appeared over my body before disappearing, causing the duvet to once again fall against me. As the duvet came back down so did the hand which, although I had fully expected to be the end result, still felt shocking as it made contact.

The second his hand met the delicate and sensitive flesh at the side of my stomach I breathed in sharply, resulting in my chest expanding and my stomach flattening as though it were trying to get away from the hand. The intake of breath was so forceful that my lungs filled and then stopped, preserving the air inside them, as though I'd forgotten the next part of the act of breathing, an act I was more than well-enough versed at to know what came next. Only when the hand met my skin again and rested still for a moment, did I have the courage to breathe out, which I did softly, to ensure my body's contact with the hand at all times.

Just as I'd grown comfortable with Mike's hand resting on my side, his fingers began to move slightly, in the same pattern they had earlier in the evening, but without the gossamer barrier of my light summer dress. This time it was not comfort that was to be derived from this action, my heart rate was not instructed to decrease as it had before, it was being coerced into rising, which it did, to the point of seeming audible to my ear. I wondered how, when I felt like my heart was going to burst from my chest at this time, I was expected to survive anything more intimate.

His fingers continued to move in small circular motions, as we both considered our next move. By not shirking away, or swatting his hand with mine, I was consenting to his touch. I wanted him to know his actions were warranted, but I was still nervous and lacking the confidence to say so, either verbally or with my own body. As the circles he made with his fingertips began to widen I felt a surge of confidence welling up inside me. The moment just one of his fingers reached the halfway point of my side, equidistant from my hip and shoulder, I involuntarily turned my head to face him and tilted slightly at the waist to bring my lips towards him. I didn't know where my lips would impact, I didn't care, all I knew was I needed to kiss him now.

My mouth didn't have far to travel, across the small gap between our pillows, until it met his. At first my lips hit just below his own, at the deep crevice between lips and chin, but he skilfully shifted down, to make sure my next kiss hit him square on its intended target. The fact that my lips had just touched his, caused me to stop for a second, as though mentally filing my first kiss into a safe area of my brain, never to be removed or overwritten. Once I had done so, I leant back in and felt the full force of his kisses, which became more fervent and applied more pressure on my lips each time.

The kisses went from gentle to firm, from ordered and symmetrical, to chaotic and at every conceivable angle. He turned his head left slightly and each kiss in this position felt new, he moved his head up and kissed with both of his lips on just my top lip, then repeated this on my bottom lip. He strayed away from my mouth and his kisses continued across my cheek, behind my left ear and down to my neck. As he did so my head tilted back, giving him a better angle and more exposed flesh for him to sample. Again I felt breathless and had to remind myself to exhale on more than one occasion.

He soon made his way back up to my mouth, kissing every inch of skin in between, before prising my lips apart with his as his kisses grew more forceful. My lips snapped shut, instinctively, but each time he tried they remained open for a little longer. Eventually, without warning, he kissed me and ran his tongue softly against the newly exposed inside of my upper lip. It provided a whole new sensation, even though it was only there for a fraction of a second, for it was warmer, softer and slightly dewy in comparison to the kisses that preceded it. I allowed my lips to open slightly more frequently and for fractionally longer each time.

Each kiss now was like its own individual love story, with a discernible beginning, middle and an end. His lips first struck mine in introductory fashion, then his tongue provided a sensual burst of action before his lips returned to close that particular chapter and leave me wanting more. We kissed like this for page after page until, quite by accident, his tongue grazed the tip of mine and we began a whole new chapter of our story. I instinctively put my tongue out again to force him to graze it, this time less fleetingly. Our mouths were now wide and we gave up on kissing motions altogether for a minute, while we explored each other's tongues with our own.

By now my neck was starting to ache from being at ninety degrees to the rest of my body for so long. As I tried to pull my head back towards my chest his head followed, not allowing me to part from him for one second. He rose up on his haunches, his hands balled into fists, pressing into the bed as he tracked my head movement exactly. His upper body now arched over me from the side, our heads at a forty-five degree angle to one another which gave a new and exciting feel to our kisses.

Acutely aware of his chest above mine, the chest I'd first seen just a few days ago in the hallway of his house, I couldn't wait any longer to touch it. I reached up my right hand and placed the palm flat against his left pectoral muscle, just above and to the side of his nipple, and left it there while he kissed me. I was pleased that I had summoned the courage to begin my own exploration of his body. His chest was taut, I found myself lightly pressing my fingertips into it just to gauge the precise firmness.

From the position we now found ourselves in, it was clear just how much he dwarfed me. His large frame towered over me in a way that ought to make me feel vulnerable, but his gentle nature assured my safety. I brought my other hand up to lay it flat against his chest, almost as if about to push him away, but never actually doing so. The palm of my left hand found his nipple, which stiffened and thus prevented me flatting my hand completely against him.

I inadvertently moved my left hand fractionally to one side, my palm gently grazing the very tip of his nipple, and causing him to provide me with my firmest kiss yet. My confidence grew exponentially knowing that I had directly caused this reaction. I kept my hand flat for a few more gentle kisses before repeating the prior action and instigating the exact same result. I enjoyed these firm kisses more than any other, but I knew that too many of them would lessen their impact, so I removed my hands from his chest altogether.

Despite my new found confidence I was still being steered through this sexual dance. I had neither the strength of body nor mind to take charge of the situation, even if I'd wanted to. I was happy to let him lead, as I believed the man should. I did sense my opportunity though, as he lifted his torso up for a moment to catch his breath. I pushed gently on his left shoulder with my right hand, not forcibly enough to move him but enough to suggest to him that he might turn over. As he lifted that left shoulder and began to turn, I kept my hand in contact with it and moved my right shoulder in sync to follow, demonstrating that this was not to be the end of the dance, merely the end of the prelude.

He lay back, flat on the bed, as I had done up to that point, and I lifted my right leg over his body and onto the mattress beside him. During this whole process I kept my lips within inches of his, I felt as though in future, I never wanted them more than this distance apart. As I sat over him I leant back in for a kiss, he placed both hands against the very top of the backs of my thighs, seeming careful to keep them below my bottom. Every time I pulled my lips away, his followed briefly, his head lifting from the pillow and his hands gripping more tightly against my legs.

I tried to shuffle my legs down the bed slightly so that I might finally get my mouth in contact with his chest, but as I attempted to move my kisses down his neck towards my goal his wrists stiffened and stopped my thighs from moving back the necessary distance.

I returned to his mouth and massaged his tongue with mine before trying again. Once again his hands and wrists remained rigid and prevented me from doing so.

I didn't know why he didn't want me to kiss his chest but I was determined not to let him stop me. I kissed him more firmly, as he had done to me those few times, then quickly reached back to grab his hand away from my leg and shuffled back as intended. It was then that I felt the precise reason why he'd been stopping me.

Suddenly his chest was the last thing on my mind. As I'd shifted back, slightly to one side, to move my mouth towards the top of his chest, my bottom – unannounced – had pressed firmly against a previously unmentioned and unconsidered part of his body. I was completely aware of what it was, and where it could be found, yet caught utterly unaware by its presence at this time.

My first instinct was to reach back and try to move it with my hand, as one would do when inadvertently sitting on a remote control on the sofa. Fortunately I overcame this instinct and realised there was nothing I could do to remove it from its current position, pressing as it was against the soft flesh of my right buttock.

I put its presence out of my mind for a moment and continued on my quest to put my lips to his chest, as I had been vying to do so since I first bumped into it on the landing. As I planted a few kisses on this firm plateau I couldn't help but return my mind to the obstacle further down the bed. It now pulsated and pressed more firmly into my bottom with every kiss I made. It was a vicious cycle, I tried to focus on his chest but every time I did so I stirred the very thing I was trying to ignore. Not wanting to push my luck or make things awkward I returned to kissing his lips and freed myself from this distraction.

By this point, my senses were overloaded, those of smell and touch combining to conjure up a fully three dimensional image in my mind, despite the darkness obscuring my sight. I hadn't fully noticed changes in temperature either and although the room was somewhat cool and the covers had been thrown back, the heat that emanated from our bodies combined to great effect. My feet would likely have been freezing, but I really wasn't aware of anything below my burning thighs.

I couldn't wait any longer, everything we'd done thus far, every step, seemed a natural progression. I didn't once in all this feel scared, nervous or shy, and certainly not like either of us was making a mistake. Being together like this was the most normal thing in the world and with this sense of justness I leant back once again to press him against me. This time I made sure I was aligned centrally so that he made contact with the partially damp cotton of my knickers, which were warmer than the patches of skin either side.

Mike instinctively wrapped his arms around my shoulders and forced my head down to one side of his, into his neck, and held me there for a few seconds.

At first I wasn't sure if I'd done something wrong, or he was preventing me from continuing, but I soon realised he was just in need of a momentary pause and a gulp of air into his lungs to steady his nerves. He kissed at my neck and mouthed the word 'OK' into my left ear, or at least I think that was what he said, his voice had a breathless quality that made it hard to distinguish. That was to be the only word spoken that night.

I pushed back against him one more time, arching my back slightly and edging up and down so that I could feel him more closely through my knickers. As I did so he pushed more firmly against me and caused me to break contact briefly as my hips spasmed forwards and then relaxed back down against him. I pushed one hand down hard into the mattress in order to release the other, then reached down one side of my hips for my knickers which I tried to shift downwards. I only pushed them an inch or so, before realising I couldn't free myself from them in this position.

Without further prompting, my companion, with his extended reach, grabbed both sides of my knickers and expertly pushed them over my hips and halfway down my thighs. He then leant sideways and pushed one side down further to my knee and yanked them over to one side to widen the leg hole. I lifted up that leg and fed it through the hole until my toes popped through, then he let go and leant to the other side to repeat the process. I relieved him of his duty and pulled the other side down myself, but only as far as my calf, where they would remain for now, attached but unrestrictive.

I didn't have the time or inclination to remove them completely, as soon as I felt free of their binding constraints I simply had to push back against Mike and feel him directly against me. Despite the minimal thickness of the barrier that we'd just removed the sensation was totally different. Such warmth and power, as if I could actually feel the blood coursing through as it pressed against me, this time edging ever closer to being inside.

I stayed somewhat still from now on, preferring not to lean back against him but instead ushering him to press against me. He repeated the motion I had done before, gradually up and down against me, spreading the warmth and wetness I had created equally across the surrounding area. Then he probed me a few times, like a boxer working his jab before the sucker punch, each time edging slightly further inside me and covering his tip in the lubricant I naturally provided for him. I clung tightly to his shoulders and closed my eyes firmly as I waited for the inevitable.

I was compelled to breathe in sharply as I felt him enter me for the first time, holding that breath as he remained an inch or so inside me, perfectly still. Only when I slowly breathed out from the initial shock did he gently ease himself partially out before heading back in slightly further than the previous time. He repeated this process of gentle exploration and marginal gains until he was as far inside me as my body would allow. During these careful, yet considered strokes, I felt every millimetre of him against the inside of me, every minute bump and ridge of the surface. I never truly knew him until now.

The physical sensation of having him inside me was indescribable. Not in the prosaic sense of the word, but rather in the literal sense that nothing I had ever experienced could come close, and thus, no words I had could accurately describe it, or give it a sense of context. The feeling was overwhelming, both my heart and head were also filled by him. I could barely breathe as he slowly started making love to me. I was dizzy, I felt all the blood had rushed away from my head, which no doubt it had. All of this was intoxicating, like a mountain climber suffering from oxygen deprivation and experiencing a magical and lucid high.

Once I'd become sufficiently comfortable with his gentle thrusting action, I was finally able to return my head upright and facing his. I was desperate for a kiss now, somehow the closeness of body we had wasn't enough, the closest we could be was with our lips locked. I leant in and kissed him gently on the lips. As I did so I could feel him pulsating and twitching inside me. These sudden movements provided new and exciting sensations, seeming to rub against new, unexplored areas inside me. I couldn't help now but pounce on him open mouthed and kiss him firmly, my tongue probing for the touch of his. As I did so I felt an even more pronounced twitch and he surged forward dramatically, actually pushing me further up the bed, my lips in line with his forehead.

He then grabbed my hips quite forcibly and pushed me back down against him, deeper than ever before. This stung a little and made me quite uncomfortable, but my inexperience permitted me to allow it. We stayed still like this for around thirty seconds before he allowed me to lift up slightly and relieve the pressure inside. He then grabbed my face, unexpectedly, with both hands on my cheeks and kissed me passionately. This was the most one-sided kiss we'd shared so far, one of unbridled passion and as I later realised, gratitude. I could still feel him inside me, but less vividly than before. Moments later he pushed his hips down into the bed and eased himself out of me altogether. He rolled me off and onto the bed beside him, such that we both lay on our sides facing each other.

He kissed me one further time in this position, before burying my head in his chest. He turned partially onto his back, from where he seemed able to breathe more easily and recuperate. With one hand on my side he continued to run his fingers around my soft skin in a clockwise motion. This had a soporific, almost hypnotic effect on me, and coupled with my brain now catching up with events and realising how late it was, I could feel myself drifting away. I had mere moments to process what had just happened, I could barely make sense of it. All I knew, was that I had experienced everything I'd ever wanted from life, I felt happier than I ever thought possible.

Chapter 25

A loud bang woke me sharply and I sat bolt upright in bed, with the duvet clamped to my bare chest, completely disoriented and unaware of my surroundings. In front of me I could just about make out the shapes of two figures, one tall, one short. I couldn't see their faces, or hear them as they spoke to me through a cacophony of noise. I screamed instinctively, whilst staring straight at the two figures, only for the shorter of the two to walk closer to me and stand at the side of the bed.

'It's ok Rebecca, you're safe now.' came a woman's voice.

'Who are you? Where's Mike?' I shouted.

'I'm WPC Alice Dixon and that's PC Robertson, you've got nothing to worry about, you've done nothing wrong, we're just here to make sure you're ok.' she replied. 'Dan, could you give us a minute?'

The taller figure left the room and pulled the door partially closed behind him, but remained standing just outside. The shorter figure, WPC Dixon, sat next to me on the bed and offered me a hug. Given the circumstances, I took it. I began to cry, I was so confused by the presence of these people, I didn't really understand why they were here. All manner of possibilities were racing through my head, none of them seemed plausible. The policewoman stood up from the bed and walked over to the door, whispered something to the policeman outside and shut it firmly.

'Shall we get you dressed?' she asked. 'Do you have some clothes in here or do you want me to get you some?'

I was suddenly acutely aware of my body and the fact I was naked under the duvet. Except for my knickers, which it seems I'd managed to pull up during the night. I took a moment to respond to the question.

'Erm, my dress is by the side of the bed I think.'

'Do you want me to get it for you?' she asked.

'No, it's ok. I can manage.' I replied, before slipping sideways out of the duvet to find it.

WPC Dixon stood by the door and turned around, to give me some privacy as I got dressed. I found my bra and socks and put those on first, before hauling my dress back over my head and pulling it down over my hips. It was quite cold in this bedroom now and I really wanted the leggings and hoodie from my bedroom, but I didn't know how to say so.

'Okay, shall we go into another room?' she asked.

'Erm, okay. Where's Mike?' I repeated.

'We're looking for him now, don't worry.' she replied.

I was more confused than ever. When I'd awoken I was roughly in the middle of the bed, but as I had felt to the side of me with my hand, the sheets were cold on either side. I didn't know where Mike had gone and the officer saying 'don't worry' only served to worry me more. Was he missing? Are they looking into his disappearance? Has there been an incident of some sort in the village? All these questions rattled around in my head but I didn't yet have the wherewithal to ask.

The policewoman opened the bedroom door, the male police officer stepped aside and I was met by three or four more faces with sympathetic smiles. All of them addressed me by name, which was extremely unusual. I smiled back nervously at each of them and followed WPC Dixon into the living room. I could see blue flashing lights through the net curtains and walked over towards the window to look in more detail.

Outside the house were two police cars, one parked to the side of Mike's blue estate car, the other behind it, blocking him in. There seemed to be a raft of people standing on the threshold of the property, at the end of the gravel driveway, peering towards the cottage eagerly. Suddenly, one of the figures pointed at me and before I knew what was happening a multitude of brilliant white flashes burst in my direction. WPC Dixon ushered me away from the window and into the armchair by the patio doors – Mike's armchair. I sat down uncomfortably, looking over at *my* armchair on the other side of the room.

'It's a little cold in here, let me see if I can find you a blanket.' she said, before shouting at a colleague to find one.

I sat staring blankly across the room, still unsure as to what was happening. WPC Dixon sat on the sofa next to me, leaning forward and repeatedly smiling at me to reassure me of my safety. The strange thing was, I'd felt perfectly safe until they'd arrived *en masse* to trash the cottage. From where I sat I could hear more police officers talking and communicating on their radios.

'Bzzt. Yes, the girl is safe, I repeat, the girl is safe. She seems unharmed. Over.'

'*Unharmed*?' I thought to myself, '*Who on earth would have wanted to harm me?*' Then an inaudible noise came through the radios which was somehow interpreted by the officer in the kitchen.

'Bzzt. Nope, no sign of him as yet, we're combing the scene for any clues as to his whereabouts. Over.'

I decided to change tack and turned to WPC Dixon in order to ask one more question.

'Why has Mike gone?'

WPC Dixon leant further forward and took my hand. Just then, the taller officer, PC Robertson, arrived with a blanket, which he handed to WPC Dixon. She unwrapped it and draped it over me on the armchair, again taking my hand before speaking.

'I know it's hard to understand right now, but the important thing is you're safe. We'll find him, don't worry.'

Once again I was more worried by being told not to worry. I was also annoyed by the understatement of it being hard to understand. 'Hard to understand' didn't quite cover the confusion I felt at that moment. The last thing *I* knew was that I'd gone to sleep, next to the man I love, the man I'd always loved, more happy and content than ever before. Then I woke up in some sort of nightmare world, with missing people, patronising police officers and the incessant noises of chatter and buzzing police radios.

'There's going to be a counsellor here very soon to talk to you Rebecca.' said WPC Dixon.

By this point I decided I hated being called Rebecca. Only twenty-four hours ago it was music to my ears, a sign of adulthood and acceptance. Now it was a formal name, read from a list, like at school being said by a teacher when I'd failed an assignment or been tardy. Why was a counsellor coming to see me? I didn't want to see a counsellor. I'd had my fill of them in the months after my mum had died. Then a terrible thought hit me, knocking the air from my lungs and forcing me to gulp more in.

'He's ok isn't he?' I asked in trepidation, fearing a negative or non-committal response.

'Who's that?' replied WPC Dixon.

'MIKE.' I shouted, annoyed at the fact I seemed to be the only one concerned for his safety rather than mine.

'I'm sure he's ok, don't worry, the counsellor will be here shortly to talk about this with you.'

I'd now given up on getting a sensible answer out of WPC Dixon. She seemed to have one primary function, to ensure my immediate safety while otherwise being as obstructive as possible. I decided to wait until this fabled counsellor arrived, in the hope that they would at least be able to tell me what was going on.

Luckily I didn't have long to wait, a middle-aged woman appeared in the doorway and PC Robertson stepped aside and pointed towards me.

'Rebecca?' she asked.

'It's Becky.' I replied, in a bad tempered tone.

'Ok Becky, I'm sorry. My name's Liz Walker, I'm the police counsellor for the local area. Can I talk to you for a bit?'

Her voice was unnecessarily soft and gentle, which grated on me slightly as it reminded me of the counsellors I had seen before. For women, they spoke and behaved so differently to my mum. I found them condescending and somewhat patronising. I feared that I wouldn't get any better answers to the questions I had spinning around my head than I did from WPC Dixon. Nonetheless I nodded to indicate my compliance in this matter. WPC Dixon got up and closed the door to the living room and sat in my armchair, which distressed me greatly.

'So Becky, do you know why we're here this morning?' asked the counsellor.

'No. Nobody will tell me anything. I want to know where Mike is. What's happened to him and why are there police here?' I replied, the words cascading out of my mouth at speed.

'Ok, well there's a limit to how much I can tell you at this stage,' she said, causing me to sneer and roll my eyes before she continued, 'but Kent police had a call from your father yesterday, he reported you missing.'

Suddenly things started to become clearer, at least some of what was happening now made sense. Although I still couldn't understand the reason for the sheer number of police that now swarmed over Ivy Cottage. They'd found me. I was fine.

'You told him you were going to stay with your friend Lucy, is that right?' she continued.

I nodded, but didn't want to expand on it, as I was aware my lie would untangle pretty quickly.

'Your father called Lucy's parents yesterday morning to check what time you'd be home today, they informed him you'd not been round at all this weekend. That's when he called the police. Is there a reason you didn't get in touch with your father after leaving on Thursday night?'

At least I had a good answer for this question.

'I picked up the wrong mobile phone, I didn't have his number with me.' I responded.

'Ok.' said the counsellor, in a fashion that suggested she was going to take everything I said with a pinch of salt. 'So instead of going to your friend Lucy's house for the weekend, you contacted Mr Rawley, is that correct?'

It took me a few seconds to realise who this Mr Rawley was. I was aware of Mike's surname but I don't think I'd ever heard it said out loud.

'Yes, that's right. I called Mike and he picked me up.' I replied.

'Ok and you've been with him since Thursday evening?'

'Yes.' I replied.

'Ok and we understand you went to London together and stayed in a hotel there for two nights, is that correct?'

I was caught a little off guard by this question. I wasn't sure how they knew we'd been to London, or now that I thought about it, how they knew to find us here in the cottage. I found it all rather perturbing that they knew so much about us and our movements. I continued to co-operate with her enquiries regardless of my unease at how the balance of power had tilted in her favour.

'Yes. We went to London, stayed in a hotel for a few nights and then came here cos Mike's friends wanted him to check on the house while they were away.' I said.

'Ok, I see, and you were willing to go to London, and again willing to come here to Ivy Cottage?'

'Erm yeah, I guess so.' I replied.

'I have one final question I need to ask you. It's very important so I want you to think carefully before you answer. Also I want you to remember that you've done nothing wrong and that you're not in any trouble. Okay?'

I nodded with a sense of terror at what sort of a question had to be prefaced in this way.

'At any time did Mr Rawley engage you in any sexual activity? By sexual activity we mean touching you either through your clothes, or under your clothes, or ask you to touch him, or any kind of act that you would consider to be sexual in nature.'

My jaw dropped and I turned bright red with embarrassment. I didn't want to tell her anything but I felt I'd be in trouble if I lied to the police. At this moment, WPC Dixon chose to stand up from her position in my armchair, walk over towards the door and wait. I was in stunned silence, I had enjoyed the most wonderful night of my life and now I was being questioned about it, made to feel like some kind of victim.

'Take your time Becky.' said the counsellor, 'You understand the question don't you?'

I nodded and quietly mouthed 'Yes'.

'Is that a yes you understand the question, or yes Mr Rawley engaged in sexual activity with you?'

'Both.' I replied sheepishly, whilst looking at the floor. I felt so violated by this line of questioning. What had previously seemed magical now just made me feel horrid.

'I'm sorry Becky,' she pressed, 'but I need you to actually say yes. Did Mr Rawley engage in sexual activity with you?'

'Yes, we had sex. We had sex last night.' I replied, before bursting into tears.

WPC Dixon opened the door and whispered something to PC Robertson again. He nodded and shuffled away down the corridor. WPC Dixon closed the door behind her, turned and smiled at me from across the room and returned to sit in my armchair.

The counsellor passed me a pocket-sized pack of tissues. I opened them and pulled one out to dab at my eyes.

'I'm sorry to have upset you. We'll need to ask you some more questions later but that's it for now.' she said.

WPC Dixon piped up from the other side of the room.

'Your father is on his way here. We'll take you to the local police station and wait there for him to arrive. Do you want me to pack up your stuff?'

The last thing I wanted was to see my father, especially when I was still worried about where Mike was. I knew I was in for one hell of a lecture when I got home. My father would probably act all polite and understanding in the presence of the police, but they'd never see the real him.

'Yes please.' I replied. 'It's all in that bedroom.' I said, pointing through the wall.

WPC Dixon left the room to collect my things. As I sat, I began to wonder about how the police were interpreting our situation. They were clearly more concerned about my welfare than Mike's, although they at least seemed fixated on finding him, now that my safety had been assured. The last thing I wanted was to get Mike into trouble, I felt like all this was my fault. I voiced this sentiment to the counsellor, who assured me that it most certainly wasn't. That didn't help assuage my guilt.

WPC Dixon returned with my little suitcase, my backpack and my wash bag from the bathroom, I packed them all up together. I was still wearing my summer dress, it felt too bright and cheery for my current mood. I wanted to change into something more comfortable but I didn't think they'd let me. Instead I brought the blanket back up over my legs and arms and continued to rack my mind for anything I was missing.

In doing so I stumbled upon the inconceivable. What if the police were right? What if it wasn't my fault? What it Mike had planned this whole weekend? Where was he now? Why had he left? Surely I couldn't have misjudged him, misread his intentions this badly? What if I *had* been the victim in all this? I certainly felt like it, all wrapped up in a police issue blanket with officers and a counsellor around me.

There was a sudden knock on the living room door, WPC Dixon walked over to open it. PC Robertson muttered something to her and she nodded, before turning to me.

'It's time to go now Rebecca. We'll go to the police station and wait there for your father. Don't worry, I'll be with you the whole way.'

I wasn't worried about the journey to the police station, I was worried about the journey away from it. I stood up, grabbed my bags and walked towards the door. As I stepped out of the living room, the extent of the operation became apparent. The police officer's conversations were louder and clearer from here. One stood in the hallway with gloves on, putting Mike's camera that I'd left there the previous afternoon into a clear plastic bag.

Just as we walked towards the front door, from where I could see more clearly the police cars parked haphazardly on the gravel drive, I heard one final audible conversation.

'Anything of any use in the bins?' said one voice.

'Not much. Just food packaging, some plastic bags and a post-it note.' said another.

'What's on the post-it note?' asked the first voice.

'Just one word.' he replied.

'MILK.'

Why not leave a review?!

If you enjoyed this book – or even if you didn't – please take the time to review it on the retailer's website. You don't have to write much, just let people know what you liked and whether you'd recommend it to others. Every review helps!

About the author

MJ Meads is the author of Milk and the award-winning short story Salvation. MJ is a keen student of the human condition and attempts to create literary works that seek to highlight changing public perception and the prevailing discourse on morality, ethics and social acceptability.

www.mjmeads.com

Printed in Great Britain
by Amazon